I0688409

Channing Blanche Mary

Zodiac Stories

Channing Blanche Mary

Zodiac Stories

ISBN/EAN: 9783744704335

Printed in Europe, USA, Canada, Australia, Japan

Cover: Foto ©Andreas Hilbeck / pixelio.de

More available books at **www.hansebooks.com**

ZODIAC STORIES

BY

BLANCHE MARY CHANNING

NEW YORK

E. P. DUTTON & COMPANY

31 WEST TWENTY-THIRD STREET

1899

To

THE SWEET MEMORY

OF

JULIA MARIA CHANNING

THIS BOOK IS

LOVINGLY DEDICATED

CONTENTS

———

ILLUSTRATIONS

BY
BLANCHE MARY CHANNING

ZODIAC STORIES.

INTRODUCTORY.

ELVASTON LODGE was a dear, hospitable, cosy old house, built of red brick, standing among the South Devon hills. A beautiful magnolia tree was trained against the front on one side of the wide porch, and a great mass of yellow-flowering jasmine on the other. The garden before the house was full of big fuschias, and glossy-leaved japonicas, and monthly-rose bushes. The garden sloped down-hill, and if you followed it you came to the place where it ended in a steep little path going down to the sea. At each end of the tiny bay was a tall white cliff, and the short stretch of water between was dazzlingly blue. When the hardy gorse hung out its golden flag on top of the cliffs in February, there was a splendid blaze of color to be seen.

The porch at Elvaston Lodge was a pleasant place to sit, and Ethelind's Aunt Ellen used to take her sewing out there on bright days, and Ethelind's grandfather, a fine-looking old gentleman with long white hair under a velvet skull-cap, used to bring out one of his many books and read aloud to her.

They were sitting thus one sunny September afternoon, waiting for Ethelind herself to arrive.

Grandpapa had just put his watch back in his pocket for the fourth time, and Aunt Ellen had said for at least the fifth time, that the train was late, when the sound of wheels was heard, and presently the dog-

cart came in at the gates and up the drive-
way with a pale little girl perched beside
William, the rosy-faced young groom.

Then there was a great deal of hugging
and kissing, and questioning, and answer-
ing, and Aunt Ellen was too tactful to re-
mark on the fact that her little niece's
eyes looked as though she had been crying, and only said that when she had taken
off her hat and jacket and brushed her hair,
she had something wonderful to show her.

" Poor little soul ! " said Grandpapa
gently, as the smiling servant-maid, Dor-
cas, led Ethelind away to her room, " She
looks sad enough."

" No wonder," replied Aunt Ellen. And
it was no wonder, for Ethelind's father
and mother had gone abroad to stay a
whole year ; and a year is a long time to
look forward to.

" We must manage to make her happy,
somehow," said old Mr. Elvaston.

" We are going to," said Aunt Ellen in

her cheery voice. "We are going to make her so happy that she will be surprised when the year is over,—it will have passed so quickly!"

When Ethelind came down-stairs, Aunt Ellen took her out to the kitchen and showed her five lovely little kittens curled up in a basket, and that was the wonderful thing!

One afternoon when she had been a few days at the Lodge, Ethelind was sitting on the floor of Grandpapa's study with a big book in her lap. The study was a very attractive room, and Ethelind liked to sit there. It had a low ceiling with a heavy oaken beam across it, as is common in old English houses, and a big fireplace, where there was generally a flicker of flame wreathing itself around a mossy log. Round-faced roses nodded at the windows, and there was nearly always a robin singing in the laurel tree near.

On the study walls hung pictures of ladies in gay riding-habits, and gentlemen in scarlet coats with brass buttons, riding horses which usually seemed taking such high fences that it must have been impossible for their riders to keep their seats.

There were all sorts of trophies from the hunt, also, and crossed foils, and a case of stuffed birds, and a stag's head with enormous antlers.

But to-day she was not looking at any of these things; she was absorbed in the big book.

" Oh, Grandpapa ! " she said after a while, " I wish you would tell me what all these creatures are ! "

Grandpapa looked up from his writing. " What are they ? Bring me your book, and let me see what you have got hold of, childie."

Ethelind brought the book over and laid it on the table beside him.

" They are the queerest pictures ! " she

said, "Is it some kind of a fairy book, Grandpapa?"

"No, dear," he said smiling, "This is an old Astronomy.   Those queer pictures represent the signs of the Zodiac."

"Z-o-d-i-a-c?" repeated Ethelind, her small face all drawn up in lines of perplexity, "What is *Zodiac*, Grandpapa?"

Grandpapa laughed.   "It would take a long time to explain the Zodiac," he said; "we should have to go back thousands of years to people who lived in very far-away countries,—to the wise men of Chaldea and Assyria, and to the Hindus; it would not interest you, my darling."

"But I want to know what the pictures mean," said the little girl.   "Here's a lion,—an awfully fierce lion; and there's a horse,—no, it's not a horse,—yes, it is; and it is shooting an arrow!   And there's some horrid kind of an animal with sharp claws,—and here are two dear little babies, just exactly alike; and oh!   there's a goat! Please tell me about them, Grand-papa?"

Mr. Elvaston drew her on his knee.

"Well, the Zodiac was supposed to be a belt or zone through which the sun travelled in the course of the year. There were twelve signs in this zone, one for each month, and these signs were groups of stars, called constellations. They had each a different name; the sign for this month is "Libra," or the scales. Do you see?"

"Y-es, pretty well," said Ethelind, "but I wanted to hear the stories about the funny creatures. You used to tell me such nice stories when I was here last year, Grandpapa; don't you remember? Could n't you tell me some now?"

Mr. Elvaston did not answer at once; he seemed to be thinking.

Ethelind laid her head on his shoulder, and watched his fine blue eyes. They had a way of lighting up suddenly when a good thought came to him, and they lit now.

"I will tell you a story for every sign as it comes round," he said, "and then you will always remember them. It will be one way to make the twelve months pass quickly, too, eh?"

"Twelve stories! How nice!" cried Ethelind. "Will you tell me the first one now, Grandpapa?"

Mr. Elvaston passed his hand gently over her hair.

"Not now, my pet," he answered; "I have an article to finish now. We will have the story to-morrow."

"Make it a long one," she begged; "and, oh! Grandpapa,—I've got such a delightful idea!"

"Let us hear it."

"Are n't twelve stories enough to fill a book?"

"Yes."

"Then, let's write all the stories down,

and get them printed, so that some other children besides me can know about the signs too.   Shall we?"

"We will see," said Grandpapa.

And this is the book of Ethelind's Zodiac Stories.

AQUARIUS, THE WATER-CARRIER.

HE sun had set over the rim of the desert. A pink flush showed where it had disappeared. Overhead, the sky was pale blue.

A little group, consisting of a man, a woman, two children, and a camel, reposed under a lonely rock whose top rose dark against the light in the west. The faces of these travellers were sad and anxious, for the younger of the two children lay fainting with fever in the mother's arms.

"Woe is unto us, Hassan," said the woman, addressing her husband, "woe is unto us that we came on the pilgrimage;

and woe be to those with whom we came—
those who have even left us to die here, and
who are themselves already at Mecca, if the
Bedouin have not stayed and slain them !"

"Speak not so bitterly, O wife of my
heart!" answered the man, laying his
hand on her head tenderly. "Thy soul is
grieved for the child. Be of good comfort ;
it may be that she will yet mend." But
though he thus sought to cheer his wife,
his face betrayed his own fears.

"Give me a draught of water !" moaned
the sick girl, turning in her mother's embrace and opening her large, unnaturally
bright eyes. The woman groaned.

"If we had but so much as one drop !"
she cried. "Thinkest thou, O my husband, that a spring is anywhere in this
wilderness?"

The man shook his head, and his dark
eyes were very sorrowful as he gazed at
the far horizon.

At this moment, the elder child rose

suddenly from his place at his mother's feet, and spoke earnestly, his beautiful young face lighting up with the glow of his thought.

"O my father and my mother—I will go and find a spring!" he said.

Both parents gazed lovingly upon him. But Hassan made reply,——

"Thou art not able to go forth alone and unguided into the desert, son; thou couldst find no water, and thou wouldst but lose thyself and see us no more."

"Heaven forbid it!" cried the poor mother, clasping the boy's hand tightly in her own. "If it is decreed that we are to die, let us die together."

"But we need not die," urged the boy. "Did not the Lord send His angel to show Hagar a fountain in the wilderness when Ishmael was like to perish? Hast thou not often told the story to Nejmeh and to me? And can He not now show me a spring? Let me go!"

"Water!" murmured the girl feebly,
"Water!"

Abdallah threw himself upon his knees,
and kissed his parents' hands.

"Let me go!" he entreated, "for if I
go not she will die!"

They hesitated. Then the mother said
eagerly,——

"A good thought has come to me, my
husband. Let Abdallah take with him my
necklace of many green and white beads,
and at every sixth step, let him drop one
upon the sand. Thus may he find his
way back to us,—or, if not, thou canst by
this means follow and find him."

"Wisely dost thou counsel, Kadijah,"
answered Hassan. "Do as thy mother
bids thee, Abdallah, and the blessing of
the Most High go with thee."

Abdallah was filled with joy at his
parents' consent. His eyes shone as he
thanked them. Then he bent down to
kiss his little sister's brow, and held out

his hand for the necklace. The man and the woman watched him as he went from them out into the waste, and a sob rose to Kadijah's lips. They could see his slight figure for some time, but after a while it vanished, and the great desert was void again.

Abdallah walked slowly along, carefully remembering to drop a bead at every sixth step, and keeping a keen watch at the same time for a water-spring. It seemed to him that he had gone thus a long way, and seen nothing like what he sought,— when suddenly, very near to him, he beheld seven tall palm trees with glistening tops which still caught the light of the sinking sun, long since lost to the lower levels. At their feet, in the midst of a circle of rich green grass, leaped a silvery fountain. Abdallah rubbed his eyes. Could it be true? Yes,—it was not a mirage, but a real water-spring. He threw himself on the ground, his forehead touching the sand, and thanked Allah for the marvel. Then he hastened to fill the water-skin which his father had given him, and stopping only for an instant to take a hasty draught himself, for his own thirst was painful, he turned back towards the distant rock with his burden. The green and white beads shone against the tawny sand, and guided his steps. But what was this?

Sitting by the way was an aged man, in ragged clothing, holding in his left hand a pilgrim's staff, while he held the right outstretched to Abdallah. His sunken eyes were fixed longingly upon the water-skin and he said faintly,—

" Stay my son! Let me drink of the water you bear, for I am parched with cruel thirst. I have yet many leagues to travel, and if I may but refresh myself I shall perhaps be able to reach my journey's end ere night falls."

Abdallah was troubled. He felt that

he ought not to delay an instant, and yet it was a duty to help the suffering, and to respect the aged.   And this old man was a pilgrim—a good, devout, old man, who certainly should not be allowed to faint of thirst. So he came near, and held his water-skin to the old man's lips, and did not complain when he took a long and deep draught, though he wished that less might have satisfied him.

"The blessing of the Most High go with thee, my son, and may He, the Merciful, grant that thou and thine never want for water," said the pilgrim.

So the boy once more fastened the skin in its place, and hastened on, picking up the scattered beads as he went.

He had just taken up the fourth bead, when, to his great surprise, he saw a black goat stretched out upon the sand before him.   Its eyes were raised beseechingly to his face, and it bleated feebly as if asking aid.   Evidently it also was in need of

water. Again Abdallah hesitated, wondering what he ought to do.   How could
he wait—how could he waste the precious

liquid he had come so far to find?   And
at the same time, how could he leave this
poor creature to die? He gave a deep
sigh, and drawing closer to the goat,
poured some water into its mouth.

2

The goat's eyes now looked gratefully up into his, and, to the boy's astonishment, it got upon its feet, and shaking its head quite friskily, sprang away into the desert.

Abdallah now made such haste to go on that he almost ran.   Darkness was falling, and he could only see the beads with difficulty.   He felt afraid that very soon he should not be able to see them at all. And his parents—what would they think had happened to him?

His steps were suddenly stayed—a fresh hindrance was to be met.   Right in his way, so that he had almost run against it, lay a gaunt, starved-looking dog. Abdallah had grown used to seeing sudden appearances, but he started at this one for he had been sure that he would not again be interrupted.   And this time he made up his mind that he would not stop to give away any more of his already diminished store of water.   Perhaps he had been foolish to give away any of it; at least he would

save the rest for Nejmeh—poor, darling
Nejmeh, who had waited all this time, and
who needed it so much ! He resolutely
shut his eyes in order not to see the unfortunate dog, and put both hands over
his ears so as not to hear it moan, and
would have passed by ; but the dog, as if
reading his thoughts, summoned up all its
weak strength, and threw itself in front of
him so that he stumbled over its body.
He opened his eyes and met the dying
animal's gaze. And he knew that it had
conquered, for he could not leave it to
perish now. With a heavy heart he
lifted its head on his knee and poured a
few drops of water down its throat ; not
many, for so little water was left by this
time !

And then, once more, Abdallah started
forth, running fast through the twilight,
panting and despairing of reaching the
high rock before the night fell, but hoping,—hoping that somehow, in some way

beyond his knowing, — Nejmeh would yet be saved from death.

But why did he come to a standstill, and raise his hand to his eyes as if the sun which had set so long before, dazzled him?

No pilgrim, no goat, no dog was before him now, but a beautiful being whose eyes shone like stars, with wings whose golden feathers swept the dust, and whose raiment was like the full moon,—so radiant in its whiteness.   Abdallah drew back in awe and was about to throw himself at the feet of the vision, but it held up a finger to check his impulse, and at the same time smiled so tenderly at him that he ceased to be afraid.

" Knowest thou me, son?" asked the bright apparition.

"Thou art one of the angels of the Most High," answered Abdallah reverently.

"And thou hast already seen me three

times this day; dost thou remember me ?"

Abdallah shook his head.

" Surely I remember thee not! When did I see thee before, thou blessed one ? "

The angel smiled yet more sweetly into the boy's wondering face.

" Yet hast thou both seen and served me," he said; " I was the aged pilgrim, and the thirsty goat, and the dying dog to which thou gavest drink. And now thou shalt never lack water to quench thy thirst and that of thy house, all the days of thy life. Thou didst not grudge to give when thou hadst need thyself; therefore is the water-skin full at thy girdle; and for the necklace—behold, it is again in thy bosom. Haste thee, Abdallah, ' Servant of God,' and the blessing of the Merciful go with thee."

Then the boy saw the angel no longer; but the high rock rose of a sudden close at hand, and he sprang forward, crying :

" My father ! my mother ! Nejmeh ! I bring you water—water from heaven ! "

To his joy, Nejmeh, looking in perfect health, ran to him, and cast her arms about his neck. Also, his parents embraced him.

Then they all praised Allah for His great mercies; and Abdallah sat at his mother's feet, and told all that had befallen since he left them, and they drank of the water and gave their good camel his fill ; and at the end, the skin was as full as at the beginning.

After which, Kadijah asked for the beads of her necklace, and at once Abdallah drew from the bosom of his tunic— not a necklace of common beads, but a string of emeralds and pearls, each one as large as a palm-seed.

Then they gave praises anew. And when it was day, they went on their journey to Mecca.

But the word of the angel was fulfilled

to Abdallah, for in the years that came after, never did he or his lack water to drink and to bestow on those who were in need thereof.

PISCES, THE FISHES.

HEY were two little Japanese, and their names were Cherry-Bloom and Plum-Blossom.

They lived with their father and mother in a pretty little house with white matting on the floors, and long, banner-like pictures on the walls called " kakemonos." The rooms were partitioned off by sliding panels of wood and paper, and near the ceiling of each was a border of beautifully-carved open-work.

Cherry-Bloom was nine, and Plum-Blossom was seven. They had round, merry faces, with small, bright eyes, running up a little at the corners; and they had been taught always to smile, whatever happened.

The Japanese are a very polite people, and they think it is impolite not to smile; so if Cherry-Bloom's mother had to reprove her for being naughty, Cherry-Bloom smiled all the time; and when a bad little boy nearly drowned Plum-Blossom's white kitten, one day, she ran away to cry, and did not come back till a pitiful little smile struggled through her tears.

Cherry-Bloom wore a sort of wrapper called a " kimono," of pink and gray, with a pink "obi," or sash, round her waist; and Plum-Blossom wore a blue and white kimono, with a blue obi. These sashes were tied in a bow, like a very big butter-fly, behind.

The two little girls had no chairs, but sat on their heels on the floor, and ate millet and fish with chop-sticks out of lacquer bowls.

When they went to bed, they put on little gowns of blue cotton, and lay down on soft quilts on the floor, with their small, sleek, black heads on wooden pillows. It sounds uncomfortable to us, but they liked it.

The village where they lived was in a very pretty part of the country. In the spring the hill-sides were covered with a mass of wild fruit blossom, and the path that went down into the valley and up again to the castle of the Dragon was white with fallen petals when the wind blew.

Now the castle of the Dragon was a place that the village children regarded with great curiosity and fear. It was an old half-ruined fort, uninhabited, and popularly believed to be the haunt of a Dragon of a terribly fierce disposition, with ten claws on each foot, (taloned), and teeth of indescribable sharpness, who would eat any one daring to come within a hundred yards of the entrance gates.

Even the grown people believed in this dreadful monster, and no one of them would have been found on the other side of the valley after sunset.

One very aged man always declared that he had seen the Dragon when he was young, and that he had had green and gold scales all over his body; that he breathed fire and smoke, and that he flew by like a streak of lightning. Most persons were sure that they had heard him bellowing on stormy winter nights.

But no one took so much interest in the Dragon as Cherry-Bloom.

She was a very courageous child, and fond of an adventure; and as she looked across the valley at the castle of the Dragon, lying in the sunlight, gray and silent and mysterious, she felt as if some spell were drawing her towards it.

One sweet spring day, when the robins were calling " Good luck ! " to each other from the trees, Cherry-Bloom went softly down the path into the valley, and ever a little more slowly, and a little more slowly, up the path on the other side, to the castle of the Dragon.

She had heard that it was unsafe to go nearer than a hundred yards, so she stopped at what she thought must be short of that limit.

There was not a sound but the chirr-irr of insects in the warm air, and the happy call of the birds. She waited ; she waited so long that she began to wish that something would happen. But nothing did.

If the Dragon were at home, he was remarkably quiet.

Perhaps he was asleep.

Perhaps he was away .

Emboldened by this idea, she went on a few steps ; then a few more, on and on, until she actually reached the big stone gateway. And still nothing happened. In a rash moment she put out a small pink hand and touched the gatepost. And then, terrified at her presumption, she fell flat on her face, with both hands over her eyes.

But the robins kept on calling, and the sun kept on shining ; and peeping through her fingers, and seeing no Dragon, she was comforted.

But she did not want to stay any longer, so getting up quickly, she turned and ran, never stopping till she had reached her own home.

"You have been away a long time," said her mother ; "do not stay so long when you go to play again."

Cherry-Bloom smiled ; but she was even then resolving to make a second trip to the castle of the Dragon.

That night, when their parents were asleep, Plum-Blossom heard her name

pronounced in a whisper. She turned
over towards her sister.

"What is it?" she said sleepily.

"Open your eyes and listen : to-morrow
I go to the castle of the Dragon!"

Plum-Blossom opened, not only her eyes,
but her mouth also, and sat up in bed.

"And you will go with me!" her sister
proceeded.

"Never!" said Plum-Blossom. "Do
I want to be eaten up?"

"That is all nonsense, that eating up!"
said Cherry-Bloom scornfully. "I was
there myself alone this morning, and was
I eaten up? No!"

Plum-Blossom gasped.

"Yes," continued Cherry-Bloom, "I
went up to the gate, and *touched* it, and
yet, you see, nothing happened to me!"

Plum-Blossom was speechless. She was
overwhelmed by her sister's courage.

"And to-morrow, I am going through
the gate,—yes, right into the garden, and

then, if nothing happens, on into the castle itself."

" Oh, but think of the Dragon !" Plum-Blossom almost wailed.

Cherry-Bloom leaned nearer and said impressively :

" I don't believe there is any Dragon !"

At this moment their mother spoke from the next room.

" Someone is talking who ought to be asleep," she said. " Do not let me hear any more of it."

So the little girls ceased whispering, but it was a good while before either of them fell asleep.

Plum-Blossom was quite resolved not to go to the Dragon's castle, but at the same time she was afraid that Cherry-Bloom the strong-willed would make her go in spite of herself ; and so it proved, for early on the following morning, two little figures, one with a pink obi, and one with a blue, might have been seen going down the path into the valley, and, after an interval of invisibility among the trees, slowly emerging on the opposite slope.

There was the old ruin, looking to Plum-Blossom so fearful in its nearness, that she threw herself down without more ado, and rubbed her little brown nose in the dust.

"O august Dragon ! O serene Dragon ! do not eat us up !" she moaned through her fingers.

Cherry-Bloom had not prostrated herself.

"Get up !" she said, "there is no Dragon here. It is safe as far as the gateway ; have I not proved it ?" And she marched on, dragging her reluctant sister with her.

"I will go no farther !" screamed Plum-Blossom, after another ten steps, " I hear the Dragon !" And down she went again, trembling with fright.

"You heard nothing," said Cherry-

Bloom calmly, "there is nothing to hear." And she dragged the younger child forward again. But three feet from the gate, Plum-Blossom got her hand free and ran back a yard or so.

"Come!" called her sister imperiously, but Plum-Blossom shook her head.

"Then I will go alone," said Cherry-Bloom, and, put on her mettle, she walked not only up to the gate, but in between the great stone posts, and out of Plum-Blossom's sight.

An utter silence followed, and the little watcher outside began to wonder if she was being eaten up. She felt nearly sure that Cherry-Bloom would have cried out if she had seen the Dragon. Still, the silence was too dreadful to be borne, and her love for her sister overcoming her fears, she ran to the gate, and entered the enchanted place.

Such a curious old garden—ruined pavilions and rare plants run riot, and little

3

dwarf trees that looked a thousand years old.

And there stood Cherry-Bloom un-harmed.

Plum-Blossom ran to her and threw both arms around her.

"I am glad that you have found your courage again," said Cherry-Bloom, "and you must keep tight hold of it, for now we are going up into the castle."

"Oh no!" pleaded Plum-Blossom, clinging to her, "Since the august Dragon has spared us, let us go home immediately!"

"Little Faint-Heart," cried her sister, laughing, but patting the black hair of the head on her shoulder gently at the same time, "The Dragon is certainly asleep or away, or he would have eaten us up before now."

As she spoke, she moved towards a flight of steps leading up to the main entrance, and, pulling the protesting Plum-

Blossom along, climbed them and stood on the threshold. The door was gone from between the great door-posts, and the children found themselves looking into a roofless court, empty and desolate, grass and weeds sprouting through the cracks in the floor. Opposite them was another open doorway, and crossing the courtyard very cautiously, for now they were in the Dragon's power if there really were a Dragon—and very softly, because (like all well brought-up Japanese) they had put off their small shoes at the outer door,—they approached the entrance.

"Let us go no further!" begged Plum-Blossom in a faint whisper. "Not a step, dearest sister, I entreat! The Dragon may be in there where it is so dark, watching us, ready to snap us up in another moment!"

Cherry-Bloom's pink cheeks turned quite white, and it is more than possible that if she had been alone she would have fled at this juncture ; but she felt it a point of honor not to let Plum-Blossom know that she was at all afraid, so she went straight up to the door and looked through.

At first she could see almost nothing. Then she perceived that this room was larger than the first, and just as empty, except for two huge vases of blue-green porcelain in the form of fishes, each standing upright on its tail, upon a heavy stone base, its big mouth so wide open that it could have easily swallowed one of the little girls.

The children's first thought naturally was that they had come upon TWO DRAGONS instead of one, and in an instant they were on their faces, waiting to be devoured. But one minute—two minutes—ten minutes passed, and nothing happened. Then Cherry-Bloom peeped through her fingers to see if the Dragons were sharpening their teeth.

The great green fishes gaped at the ceiling as blankly as ever.

She got up softly, so far as to sit back on her heels, ready to fall on her face again at the least movement of the monsters, but there was not any.

Then she plucked Plum-Blossom by the sleeve.

" Get up," she whispered, " They are only porcelain ; there is nothing to be afraid of ! "

Plum-Blossom peeped through her fingers in her turn.

" Truly ! " she murmured in a moment more.   Then the little girls got on their feet, and to make perfectly sure, went up to the fishes, felt of them, and looked down their throats.

" I have an idea ! " said Cherry-Bloom. " If we hear the least sound, as if any one were coming, we can jump into one of these fishes and be hidden.   Is n't that a good thought ? "

"Splendid!" said Plum-Blossom; and then being little girls,—and Japanese little girls in particular,—they began to giggle, because it really did seem such a funny scheme. Only ten minutes before they had been shaking with fear, and now they were shaking with laughter.

They laughed till they cried.

"Suppose we could not get in?" suggested Plum-Blossom with sudden doubt.

"Of course we can get in," replied her sister, "and to prove it we will get in now."

"Oh no, I don't want to!"

"You always don't want to!" said Cherry-Bloom. "Just do as you see me do."

"But suppose we could n't get out again,"—timidly.

"Suppose—suppose! Now look at me!"

Cherry-Bloom mounted on the stone base, and climbing with some difficulty

up the big fish's back, put both feet into
its wide mouth, and slid down inside.

Plum-Blossom gave a gasp which was

almost a sob.   Was Cherry-Bloom killed?
No; for her round, smiling face appeared

in a moment more, framed in the dolphin's mouth.

" Do just what I did," she said in a loud whisper. Plum-Blossom tried to obey, but she was smaller than her sister, and not so active.

She slipped off the shiny back two or three times, and when at last she succeeded in getting her feet into the fish's mouth, she slipped down too quickly, and Cherry-Bloom could hear her muffled sobs from within the vase.

She was about to call out " Have you hurt yourself ?" when another sound struck her quick ears,—a sound of feet— of heavy, grown-up feet ; and in a moment she had uttered one loud " Hush !" for the benefit of her little sister, and crouched down lower in the body of the china dolphin. And now she made a discovery.

There were two holes in the fish— small, round holes, one on each side, perhaps to indicate gills—and out of these one could peep without being seen.

She put her eye to the right-hand hole, from which she could see the other fish, and made another discovery : there were holes in that one also, and she was sure that Plum-Blossom's eye was looking out of the nearest one. She took her face from the aperture, and put a finger through and wiggled it. Then she put her eye back, very quickly, and saw, as she had expected, Plum - Blossom wiggling her finger !

There was no time for another signal, for now the feet were growing louder, and the Dragon himself might be coming, after all.

Up the steps they came, then there was a pause; and then she could hear them again, crossing the outer court.

The doorway by which they had entered was opposite the fishes, and now they saw, framed in it, a figure almost as startling as the Dragon himself. It was that of a short man, clothed in a striped upper garment of black and yellow, and lower garments which the children took to be white cotton bags. But if the dress of the stranger was so odd as to be disquieting, far more so was another thing they instantly observed,—his hair, which ought to have been black, like the hair of all their acquaintances, was of a bright and blazing red !

Now, it is well-known in Japan, that no one has *red hair*, but the sake-demons, who live in wild, remote places, and drink more rice-wine than is good for them.

Cherry-Bloom and Plum-Blossom had often heard of these curious beings in the fairy-tales familiar to Japanese children, and had thought of them as harmless, good-natured creatures, not fond of eating little girls ; oh, no,—but suddenly to be brought face to face with one a long way from home, was decidedly discomposing ;

and so they cowered down inside the big fishes, and trembled; not knowing what might happen to them if they were found. That the intruder was a sake-demon, they had no doubt.

The sake-demon looked round the dusky space, and said something to himself in a strange language which the children had never heard before. Then he advanced slowly across the room, towards the fish in which Cherry-Bloom was hidden. He stood so close to it that she could hear his breathing, and she thought he must hear her heart beat. But he did not seem to. He evidently admired the fish, walking around it, and studying it with interest; but to her joy he did not look into its mouth.

Presently, he turned away from the fish, and went up to a door which Cherry-Bloom had meant to examine after a while, if she had not been interrupted, and tried to open it. It seemed very tightly closed;

he tugged and pushed till his face grew red. At last it gave way, and a great shaft of light came through the darkness, for the door led into another roofless enclosure like the outer court.

The flying open of the door with a loud noise, startled Plum-Blossom, and she uttered a small scream. It was a very small one, but the stranger heard it. He glanced quickly at the left-hand fish, and then, at one stride, was beside it. The next instant he was gazing down its throat, and the next, he had stretched his hand into its depths!

Cherry-Bloom could bear no more. With a scramble and a flop she was outside her dolphin, and down on the floor, with her hands outstretched in supplication.

"O! most honorable Sake-Demon! O Benevolent One!" she wailed, "do not hurt my sister!"

Plum-Blossom now screamed at the top

of her voice; and the sake-demon looked petrified with amazement.

"Well, if ever any one saw the like!" he said in English, adding in Japanese,— "Do not be afraid, my children, I will not hurt you."

He repeated this in a still more reassuring tone, and Cherry-Bloom, always quick to recover her courage, now peeped at him between her two fingers to make sure if he really meant what he said.

He saw this and smiled at it.

"Get up, little sister," he said gently; "Of what are you so much afraid?"

Cherry-Bloom sat back on her heels, and looked at the fish from which she knew Plum-Blossom's eye was watching, but said nothing.

"Is it because I am a stranger?"

Still silence.

"Oh, come now, what is it?" he continued, "I had no idea I was so appalling a person!"

Cherry-Bloom gave a gasp, but her politeness rose to the occasion ; she must answer.

" The honorable dress of the August One is not what we are accustomed to seeing," she stammered.

The August One looked down at himself.

" A striped blazer and white ducks— I suppose it *does* strike the native mind as odd," he said to himself in English.

Cherry-Bloom was afraid that she had offended him, and threw herself at his feet afresh.

" The clothes of the Serene Sake-Demon are all-magnificent!" she said, " They dazzle my miserable eyes!"

The young man burst into a fit of laughter.

" What in the world do you take me for?" he asked as soon as he could speak. " Did you call me a *sake-demon ?*"

Cherry-Bloom knocked on the ground

with her already dust-begrimed forehead
in assent.

" What for ? "

" Because no one has red hair like that
of the August One, except he is a sake-
demon : the August One is aware of this."

Whereupon the stranger laughed so
loud that the children were more sure
than ever that he was used to living on
sake, which is apt to make people noisy.

He soon recovered himself, however,
and trying to speak gravely, said—

" Know, O maiden ! that I am not a
sake-demon, but only a man so unfortunate as to have been born with red hair."

"The words of the Illustrious rejoice
us," said Cherry-Bloom with exquisite
politeness.—" Have we now the gracious
permission of the Illustrious to depart ? "

"Oh, no—please don't go yet !" cried
the young man. For he was an artist,
and it had struck him that Cherry-Bloom
would make a charming sketch in her

pink-and-gray kimono, if only he could coax her to pose for him.

"You have not told me yet why you and your sister are hiding in these monster dolphins. Do you live in them? Are you water-sprites?" A Japanese, old or young, is quick to take a joke, and Cherry-Bloom smiled at the suggestion. She only shook her head, however; it was as well not to tell everything. The young man had enough tact not to repeat a question which it was evident his little new acquaintance preferred not to answer. So he tried another method.

"Let us go out into the garden," he said affably; "your sister must be tired of staying in the vase; I will help her out."

Suiting the action to the word, he advanced towards the fish from whose mouth Plum-Blossom's face was now timidly peeping, but she instantly disappeared, and he saw that her fears were by no means allayed. Cherry-Bloom ran up to the fish, and whispered through the hole at some length, and then Plum-Blossom's face appeared again, and before the artist could renew his offer of help, she had placed her hands in her sister's, and was out on the floor beside her.

"Well, if you two are n't the prettiest little Jap dollies! I 'd like to stand you up on a shelf!" he said to himself in English.

"Come!" he added in Japanese, "let us go out into the air; it is dark and hot in here."

The children followed him in silence, walking hand-in-hand, and softly gathering up their small shoes as they passed through the outer doorway. The young man turned to them as they stood on the steps above him.

"Now," he said persuasively, "you are not afraid of me, are you? I don't look so very terrible, do I?"

The little girls smiled.

"I thought not! And now I want you to do me a kindness, my little sisters. I want you to stand on the step there, just where you are, and let me make a picture of you. Will you?"   .

Cherry-Bloom smiled at Plum-Blossom, and Plum-Blossom smiled at her. They looked perfectly pleasant and obliging.

"Good little sisters!" said the artist approvingly. "I will go and get my drawing materials; wait."

Poor, unsuspecting artist! He did not know those two bright little Japanese! So he was surprised when, returning a few minutes later with his easel unstrapped, his sketching-block uncovered, and his pencils and brushes in hand, he found not a trace of his models!

He stepped quickly back into the ruin to see if they had gone indoors again; he ran to the big fishes and looked down their wide mouths, which seemed to be laughing in his bewildered face.

Then he went back to the garden, and looked down the little path winding away under the wild fruit-trees, and there, just disappearing in a cloud of white branches, he saw a streak of pink and a streak of blue,—the last of Cherry-Bloom and Plum-Blossom, as they fled away to their home on the other side of the valley.

ARIES, THE RAM.

BLACK RIDGE DICK had lost his way.

He knew well the mountain-range, and when he went out to hunt that day, he had had no doubt of finding again his lonely shanty before night—but here he was, far up among the great jagged rocks on a high peak, and here was the red of the splendid sunset burning itself out in the sky, and below—slowly creeping up the long slope—was night.

Dick did not mind being alone. For a long time he had liked it best, and had built his log hut out of the way of other people on purpose. He had nothing to do with his kind except when he took a load of skins down to sell to the trading-merchants in the distant settlement.

But to be alone in the log hut, with a good supper on the table, and the door close shut, and a warm bed to go to by and by, was quite a different thing to being alone on a mountain-side, with snow coming.

For Dick knew what the great gray clouds rising as the sun set, meant.

Well, there was no help for it.   He was not very far from the timber-line, and he must build a fire before it grew dark.

He took his hatchet and went down a little way to where he saw some dead pine trees, and chopped an armful of wood.

He built his fire skilfully, and set it blazing, and then he sat down against a rock and watched it.

He had a little food with him, and he ate half of it, keeping the rest for break-fast.

When he had finished, it was dark.

He lit his pipe. All around, into the thin air, the sharp crests of the mountains rose.

Every now and again he threw on fresh fuel, and the long yellow tongues of fire sprang up, and showers of scarlet sparks were scattered on every side.

It was very solemn alone up there in the stillness. The man felt as if the fire were a comrade, watching with him.

He drew nearer to it, leaning forward to gaze into its glowing depths. He began to see pictures there.

First, the picture of his mother. Her gentle face seemed near enough to kiss. He saw a little boy kneeling by her, with clasped hands, to repeat the prayer, " Our Father who art in Heaven."

Then came another picture—the same mother-face, older and thinner, and the same boy, grown tall and strong, and an open garden gate, through which the boy was going out into the unknown world.

He could hear the gentle voice saying, "Don't give up your prayers, Dick!"

Picture followed picture—memory followed memory. Sad enough, some of them.

His life looked poor and bad in the retrospect. He had not heeded the words of kindly friends. He had grown hard and rough and selfish,—and now—

He started, and found that he had been asleep, and that the fire had burned low. As he hastened to mend it, a soft, cold touch came on his hand,—then another, and another. He looked up at the sky, and saw that the stars were no longer visible. The snow had come.

Dick shook his head.

" Going to be a big storm, I 'm afeared," he muttered. " Wonder how long I 've been asleep, now ?"

He piled more sticks upon the fire, wrapped his thick coat tightly about him, and lay down to sleep again.

From time to time he waked, always finding the snow falling, falling, still.· By daylight, several inches had fallen, covering the pine stumps, and making it harder than ever to know the way home. And still it came down, a mist of tiny white feathers which showed no sign of ceasing.

Dick dared not leave the shelter of the rock for the open. So he gathered more wood for his fire, ate the remains of the food on which he had supped the evening before, and resigned himself to wait.

It was with a gloomy face that he surveyed the ever-drifting snow, for he knew what it would mean to be " snowed up."

He pulled at his pipe, and watched the fire, and kept it bright. And so the day dragged on, and night fell again. He made up his mind that he must not let sleep overtake him to-night. He must, and would, keep awake, or he might be frozen to death.

He piled the long branches on his fire,

and sat as near it as he could with safety,
his eyes fixed upon the leaping flame.
But it was not easy to resist the drowsy
feeling which was stealing over him. His
head drooped forward, his eyelids fell over
his eyes. He slept.

When he woke, the fire was a mass of
glowing coals, but the flames had sunk.
He rubbed his eyes, shook back his hair,
and stared. For he was no longer alone.
Something living and breathing was standing on the other side of the fire, staring
back at him with bright, unblinking eyes.

Dick had not been a hunter for years
in vain, and he recognized the creature
for a large and splendid Rocky Mountain
ram.

The Rocky Mountain sheep are like no
flocks of the plains. Wild, shy, strong,
and beautiful, they dwell in the high re-
gions where few can follow them.

Dick had shot many a one, and now, after his first minute of absolute surprise,

his hand went swiftly to the leather belt where he carried his pistol and his knife. His rifle lay just out of reach.

But he paused.

The creature stood fearless and confident on the other side of the fire, its gray fleece reddened by the glow, its steadfast, untamed eyes fixed upon the hunter from between the sweeping curve of its powerful horns.

Possibly it had never seen a man before. At all events, it trusted him. It, like himself, was lost—a lonely being, snowed up, shut away from its kind ; they were companions in trouble.

Dick withdrew his hand from his belt with a shamefaced feeling as if the sheep must have understood his intention.

But it did not seem so.

After staring at him a few moments longer, it laid itself down quietly, as if used to the situation.

" Poor old fellow ! " said the man softly.

" Going to keep me company, are you?
Well, I 'll not touch you. We 'll watch it
out together."

He set his pipe going again, and made
up the fire as noiselessly as might be, and
settled himself once more.

He dozed once or twice, and waked
again. Always the mountain-sheep lay
as he had last seen it, with intent eyes
gazing into the storm.

The flock from which it had strayed
were in need of its leadership, it might
well be. Perhaps the ram knew it. Dick
wondered if it did. He wondered if animals ever thought,—if they felt things,
and knew joy and sorrow.

It was a new idea to a man whose only
view of them had been the hunter's ; who
had never loved them, but only killed
them for what they could bring him.

He noticed that one of the ram's horns
had been injured, and that the end was
broken in a peculiar way.

"I 'd know you, partner, if we met again," he said under his breath.

At last he fell into a longer sleep than he had yet experienced, and when he woke at last the sun was shining in a clear sky of pure and dazzling blue.

The snow was gone.

So was the Rocky Mountain ram. Stiff with cold, the man stood up and shook himself, and gazed about him. All around, the sharp peaks rose white and dazzling in the early sun. The last embers of the big wood-fire burned in the gray ashes.

When Dick made his laborious way home to the little shanty, one of his first acts was to open the box where he kept his few treasures, and to get out the yellow-leaved old Bible his mother had given him when he had left her years before.

There was a verse he wanted to find, and he turned the pages over, looking for it. At last a pencilled line caught his eye—ah! yes—here it was.

"'All we like sheep have gone astray; we have turned everyone to his own way'; ("Yes, that's me all over," said Dick to himself as he read,) "'and the Lord hath laid on Him the iniquity of us all.'"

"His own way" had not been quite what as a boy he had thought it was going to be. It had been a poor way,—a way taking him farther and farther from the gentle mother at whose knee he had prayed. And there was a better way than his own had been,—God's way. God would forgive the past. God could make him a better man—a man that weak things could trust.

Dick went down on his knees with his face on the faded leaf of the old Bible.

When the beautiful Indian summer came to an end that year, and the hunters came down from the mountains with their trophies of skins and horns, two of them, overtaken by night, put up at Dick's shanty.

They showed their spoils proudly.
Amongst the rest, a ram's head with one
strangely twisted horn.

Dick's hand caught at it.

"How did you get this?" he asked
eagerly.

"Shot him up yonder," said one of the
men, surprised at his excitement.

"I'm right sorry."

" What for ? "

" Because he and I were partners once,"
—and he told the story.

" I know it 's the same by the horn," he
added at the end.   " And now I want to
buy the head.   I 'll give you a fair price;
—I 'm thinking of going back East, and I
want to take this with me."

He opened a deer-skin pouch, and
poured out a heap of bright silver on the
pine table.

The rough hunter pushed it away.

" Put up your shiners ! " he said gruffly.
" You can have the head and fleece and
all.   Think I 'd sell a man *his friend's
body ?* "

And the ram's head hangs on the wall
of Dick's house in the little village where
he was born, and his children beg for the
story of how he and the Rocky Mountain
ram kept watch together in the storm.

TAURUS, THE BULL.

NCE upon a time there was a little girl named Tophra. She lived in Egypt, not far from the city of Memphis,—a great and renowned city which King Menes had built long before on the dry bed of the river Nile, after turning it into a new channel.

King Menes must have been a very clever man, but he lived so extremely long ago that we will not trouble about him here. Tophra lived about two thousand years ago, and that is quite long enough.

In spite of the two thousand years, however, she was a real little girl.

She had an oval, olive-tinted face, with

long, black eyes, and a rosy mouth which
showed two rows of small white teeth
when she laughed.   She wore her straight
black hair cut square across her forehead,
and a band of ribbon around it—or sometimes, a garland of flowers.   Her long,
scant gown fell to her little brown feet,
on which she wore gold and green shoes
of the tinest size.

Tophra was just as fond of dolls as any
little girl to-day.   She had several, made
of wood, whose arms and legs moved by
pulling a string.   The largest wore a dress
of green silk, and Tophra carried it in
her arms one beautiful summer day as
she walked in her father's garden.

A tall black nurse walked beside her,
carrying a scarlet umbrella to keep off
the hot sun.   It spread over the child's
head like a great, full-blown poppy, and
cast a glow over her pale blue gown.

Tophra's father who was named Techo,
was one of the King's high officials.   He

s

was a rich man, and on his fine estate in the fertile Nile valley, he had wide gardens, besides artificial lakes, and stables for horses and cattle.

As Tophra walked between the beds of brilliant blossoms, Samis, the chief herdsman, approached her.

"Greeting, little lady!" he said with an obeisance. "Will not my little lady like to see the new bull-calf in the cow-house? 'T is the prettiest I ever saw, sleek as silk tissue and black as night."

Tophra clapped her hands.

"Bring it to me!" she cried impetuously.

But Samis shook his head.

"That may not well be, for it is too young yet to leave its mother. If my little mistress would see it, I will carry her on my shoulder to the cow-house. The stable-yard is too miry for those golden shoes."

Tophra liked Samis, with his good-natured black face, and was willing to mount on his broad shoulder. The nurse followed laughing and protesting, as he led the way, down the flower-walk, past the lotus-pond, where the pond lilies basked in the sun, each on its pad; then through a gate, and into the stable-yard.

The nurse exclaimed discontentedly as she drew her cotton skirts higher about her ankles, and picked her way across the muddy stones, but Tophra rode high and dry on the herdsman's shoulder, her small golden shoes sparkling in the sun, and Samis was used to treading anywhere on his bare feet.

"Behold!" he said proudly, as they entered the cow-house and stopped before the largest stall.

Tophra leaned forward to look.

There in the straw lay a beautiful white cow, and beside her, a tiny calf, black as jet but for a three-cornered white spot on its forehead.

"The finest bull-calf ever I saw," said Samis. "A prince of calves—a very Rameses of calves. Is not that a sight worth seeing?"

"Oh, how soft—how small!" cried the little girl. "Can I have him in my house to play with when he can leave his mother? Can I, Samis?"

"In the house indeed!" laughed Katuki, the nurse. "Scarcely can you, Tophra."

"But you can see him as often as you will," said Samis. "I will carry you on my shoulder as I do to-day."

"I want him to play with," repeated Tophra, "and I know my father will not say 'no'; he never refuses me what I want."

Which was quite true. Tophra was the only living child of a family of five, and her parents indulged her much.

"I want to pat you, little calf," she said now. "Hold me nearer, Samis."

The man held her over the stall, and she reached down her hand towards the little bull's head. As it hovered over his nose, he suddenly put out his pink tongue and licked it, at which Tophra quickly drew it back.

"There is nothing to be afraid of," said Samis, smiling. "It is a good omen. The calf likes you."

The first person who met the child and the nurse as they re-entered their house after the visit to the stable, was Techo.

Tophra dropped the jointed doll which she had been absently dragging by one foot since its charms had been eclipsed by those of the little bull, and running to him, clasped her arms about his knees.

The tall man stooped and raised her in his arms, by which means his stern, dark face and her round, soft one were brought upon a level. He kissed her again and again, until, gently pushing him away, she said,—

"Oh, my father! I have something to ask of you. Let me speak."

Techo seated himself upon a chair of inlaid wood, and placed her upon his knee.

"Say on, most powerful Princess. What is your will?"

She was too deeply in earnest to smile.

"Concerning the bull-calf," she said breathlessly,—"it is a beautiful calf, black as night, soft as my feast-day dress,—very small. Almost small enough to go to sleep in my kitten's bed. And its eyes are so large, father; as large as *that!*"

She brought her right thumb and forefinger into a circle.

"Wonderful!" said Techo, laughing.

"Also, he has a white spot on his forehead shaped—*so.*" She stretched out the left forefinger, and brought the right forefinger and thumb against it so that they formed a " V."

"That is strange," said Techo in a new tone. He looked suddenly interested.

" Black—with the three-cornered white mark—the priest must see that," he murmured.   Then he rose and set his little daughter upon her feet.

" Run to your play, dearest : I must go."

But Tophra clung to his robe.

" Father—I did not finish about the calf.   I want it to play with."

" My child, I cannot tell whether or not I can give it to you till I have seen it."

She looked after his tall figure as he strode away, puzzled, the tears in her eyes.

" I want it for my own," she whispered, —" for my very own."

She did not see her father again that day, nor until the evening of the day after, when he came to bid her good-night.

" Father—where have you been all this time?" she cried, pulling him down to her as she lay on her little carved couch on the flat house-roof, where the Egyptians liked to sleep in hot weather, a painted awning on pillars above their heads.

"Your father has been very busy. What news do you think I have to tell you?"

"I do not know."

"Wonderful news. Will you guess it?"

"Is it about the black calf?" She sat up and twined her slender arms around him.

"It is about the black calf."

"He is to be mine to play with!" she laughed joyously.

Techo smiled gravely down upon her.

"Not that, little daughter. He is not as other calves—this creature. Tophra, do you remember the day when we all fasted and mourned because the Apis, the sacred bull Apis, was dead?"

Tophra nodded.

"All Memphis mourned," continued her father; "I saw the burial of the Apis. His immense coffin was drawn to its resting-place upon a sledge, and all the priests of Osiris followed him in garments of leopard-skin—garments of state. Do you know why they mourned so for him, little daughter?"

Tophra was not sure she knew. She had a vague notion that the bull Apis was holy, but *why*, she was not clear in her mind.

So Techo, putting an arm tenderly about

her, and speaking as fathers and mothers do of high things it is good for their children to know, told her what the people of Egypt believed; that Osiris, the kind and beautiful Sun-God, had taken the earthly shape of a black bull, marked in a special way, and that the Apis was this bull.

" And now, do you see what I am coming to ? " he said.

" You mean — oh, father—you *don't* mean——"

" I mean, little one, that the priests who have for months been seeking a new Apis, have found him at last, and that he is your black calf with the white mark on his forehead. I brought them to see him this morning, and after due examination they found, besides the white spot, two sorts of hair in his tail, and the form of an eagle upon his back, and a beetle-shaped lump under his tongue. He is Apis."

Tophra did not speak. She was afraid to say that the uppermost thought in her mind was sorrow because now the little calf could never be hers.

Techo easily guessed her thought.

" You must rejoice, little one, for now is Osiris again present with his children.

And do not grieve because the black calf
must go away.   Some day you shall have
another one for your own."

" Must this one go away ? "

" He must go to the home of the sacred
bulls so soon as he is old enough to leave
his mother.   He will be very happy there."

Tophra thoughtfully drew her little
hand down her father's face as it bent to
hers.

" I would have made him happy,—I
also," she said with a sigh.

Techo kissed the small fingers as they
played with his beard.   He was sorry for
her disappointment.

" He liked me, too ; Samis said so.   He
licked my hand when I tried to pat him."

Techo was filled with delight, seeing in
this incident the special sign of the favor
of Osiris.

" Much are you honored—much shall
the holy ones bless you," he said, laying the child back gently on her pil-

lows. "Sleep, little Tophra, and wake refreshed."

Techo's was already a famous name in Memphis, but now all men crowded to do him reverence. He with whom Osiris was pleased to abide was a man worthy of all honor.

He made a great feast for his friends in honor of the discovery of Apis, and Tophra, watching from the roof, saw the arrival of his guests.

It was high noon when they began to appear—gentlemen in chariots with servants running beside them as they drove, and ladies reclining in *palanquins* borne by slaves.

In the banqueting room, the ladies sat at one end, the gentlemen at the other; and presently a band of music began to play while they waited for the dinner to be served.

As each guest sat down to table, servants anointed him or her with perfumed ointment, crowned them with flowers, and presented a lotus to be held in the hand.

As fast as the flowers drooped in the heat, fresh ones were brought.

Slaves, standing behind the chairs, cooled the air with feather fans.

In the midst of the festivity, a hush fell on all, as two slaves came through the room, bearing the painted mummy-case of one of the family, and set it upright at the table.

This curious custom was common with the Egyptians, and in no way spoiled their enjoyment as it might ours.

After the dinner was over, and the guests had left the board, a troop of swarthy jugglers poured in, and the twang of harps and lyres, the quick clash of tambourines and sweet fluting, began again.

Tophra wished that she were old enough to be with the company. It must be very amusing. She watched the grooms waiting in the sun-scorched courtyard, and saw the chariots and litters come by and by to take their owners away, and then, being drowsy with the heat, she fell asleep with the jointed doll in her arms and the kitten curled up at her feet.

Every day she made Samis carry her to see the black calf. He grew larger and handsomer as the days passed. His tiny horns, which had looked like little knobs at first among the short curling hair of his forehead, grew longer, and his legs, which seemed weak and shaky at the beginning, were shapely, sturdy supports now. He could lash his sleek ebony sides with that slender tail, too, and after a while he could eat the food of grown-up cattle, and was pronounced old enough to leave his mother.

Then the priests fixed the day for his journey to Memphis, and every one prepared to see the procession, and to join in the rejoicings.

It was a real Egyptian day, with a
burning sun and a sky of intense, cloudless blue. Not a breath stirred the palm
leaves, and the shadows lay purple-black
against the white glare.

Little Tophra, wistfully gazing from her
roof-chamber, saw the long line of the
procession wind up from her father's
gates, out upon the road, under the palm
trees, and away towards the city, a wavy
line of black and yellow, the priests of
Osiris in their robes of leopard-skin; and,
in their midst, the young bull, walking
solemnly, proudly, as though he felt himself the centre of attention.

Hundreds of people were gathered together at Memphis for the seven-days
festival in honor of Apis. The city was
full, and the sun shone on splendid dresses,
rich uniforms, gold and silver and jewels,
glancing arms, and gilded chariots.

Through the crowds paced the Apis
with his escort. His large eyes wandered

from side to side as the people pressed forward to greet him, but he showed no fear. On and on, on and on, till they reached the state home of the sacred bulls, where were spacious courts and walks, all his own, and where two stables stood with open doors awaiting his choice.

And now Apis paused, lashing his tail, snuffing the air, seeming to consider which he would enter.

And the people held their breath, no one speaking or moving, because they believed that if he chose one stable, good fortune would follow, while if he chose the other, war, pestilence, or famine was coming upon the land.

The young bull stood, with all those eager eyes upon him, calm and unmoved. Then, just as the strain grew painful, he turned his broad head towards the stable of happy omen, and with a quickening step entered its doors and was hid from sight.

There were glad and thankful hearts in

Egypt that night.   Osiris was again in a visible shape among his children.

There were to be rich harvests in the wide Nile valley, and health and prosperity and peace.

Only a child, lying on a carved bed under a painted ceiling, cried herself to sleep for a joy that was not to be hers—for a black calf that had grown to be a bull and gone away to the city of the Apis, where he could never know how happy she would have made him with kisses and soft strokings and garlands of flowers.

And Apis himself? We cannot tell if he dreamed of Tophra and the white mother cow, as he lay in the stately stable, two thousand years ago.

6

GEMINI, THE TWINS.

HE Manse of Kirk-Andrew was a severe-looking house, over whose walls of gray granite, no playful creeper had presumed to climb. It had a square, wellkept garden in front, with a few strictly-pruned bushes in it, and two pine trees, one on either side of the gate, like sentries. A sedate white cat of uncertain age sunned herself on the doorstep of the Manse, on warm afternoons, and a redcheeked woman came to the door at intervals. A tall, very thin gentleman also was to be seen coming down and again going up the straight little path from the door to the gate. And that was about all the sign of life outside the gray old house. A stranger's first thought might have been " there are no children at this place," and there were none.

But one day the bent-backed little mail-carrier, who trudged so many miles every day that he had become a sort of walking machine, brought the minister a letter which changed the face of life for him.

He was in his study—a stern-looking room, with stiff, uncomfortable chairs set firmly back against the walls, and a big square table with a faded brown cloth on it, a huge inkstand in the centre of the cloth, and a pile of books beside it—when Eppie, the red-cheeked Manse housekeeper, took it to him.

The minister's pale face grew paler as he read that letter, and presently he laid it down on the table and laid his head on it ; and two tears ran over his thin cheeks and blotted the black-edged page.

For the letter told that his only sister —his dear sister Annie, had gone out of this world, leaving her two little boys alone.

His sister had married an Englishman, and had lived in England, and the minister had not seen her for a number of years, for he was not fond of taking journeys, and he had never seen her boys since they were small babies in arms. He remembered that Annie had begged him to visit her, many times, and he was very sorry now that he had put off doing so. Dear Annie ! What merry times he and she had had together in the grim old Manse ! It had never seemed empty and still when Annie was there ; when her sweet voice was singing upstairs and down, and all the dark corners were lit up by her sunny presence !

The minister sat in the quiet room a long while ; sometimes his lips moved

silently, for he was praying.   At last he
rose and went out into the passage, and
called "Eppie!"

The housekeeper came, wiping the flour
from her hands, for it was baking-day and
all the air was full of a warm and home-
like smell.

"Eppie," said the minister, "the Lord
has been pleased to send me heavy sorrow.   My sister Annie is gone."

Eppie raised her hands and let them
fall at her sides again.

"His will be done!" said the minister
solemnly.

"Ay! His will be done!" echoed the
woman.   "But, Minister," she added in
another tone, "what about the bairns?"

The minister looked at her with a
furtive glance, for he did not know how
she would take what he had to tell her on
this head.   Eppie was not fond of children, and she was very fond of what she
called a decent, quiet-like house; the

sort of house hard to keep up with a pair of nine-year-old boys in it. And the minister was rather afraid of Eppie, whose displeasure he always preferred not to arouse. But tell her soon he must, and the sooner the better, perhaps ; so, trying to seem at his ease, he said in a constrained voice, "The laddies are to live with us, Eppie."

A silence full of expression followed on the announcement. The minister fidgetted ; silences on his housekeeper's part were the sign of coming storm. He hastened to speak again.

"Their father having died three years ago, and his parents and near kith and kin all being gone, there is no one else but myself. I am appointed their legal guardian until they come of age."

Eppie had been making tucks in her apron, with redder cheeks than usual, but as yet she had not spoken a word. Now she heaved a sigh.

"Till they come of age!" she repeated,— "that'll be twalve year. Eh,
Minister, but Ise sorry for ye!"

The minister started. Set before him so
clearly, the prospect made him a little
sorry for himself; but he put the mo-
mentary weakness by.

"Eppie, my woman," he said gently
and yet firmly, "this is a hard thing for
you, I know well. But the Lord has sent
me a new task, and I have no choice but
to do it. If you find you can't thole the
bairns about the house, why, you must
e'en go your ways; but I've a notion
that you'll take more kindly than you
think, to Annie's lads."

"Annie's lads"—the simple words went
straight to the woman's heart, and, for the
first time in many years, Eppie broke
down and cried.

The minister cleared his throat, and
walked to the window. After a minute
or two he said quietly, "I'll be taking

the night train south.   You might put a
few things in my bit bag."

Eppie passed her apron hastily across
her eyes, and disappeared.   And the
minister knew that as far as his housekeeper was concerned, there would be
nothing to fear.

A week after the minister went away,
he came back, bringing the boys with him.
They arrived in the afternoon, tired with
their long journey, and only kept up by
the cordial attentions of Jock Bruce, the
stage-driver, who had regaled them with
red and white peppermints, and told them
fearsome Jacobite tales of the neighbor-
hood, as they sat on the box at his side.

Eppie ran out to meet them, and as
soon as she looked at them, she cried—
" Eh ! but the brown-eyed ane 's awfu'
like Miss Annie !"   And then she put her
arms around both boys and kissed them.
They drew back as soon as they could,
politely, but the " brown-eyed one " looked

up into Eppie's face and smiled respons-
ively.

"I know who you are," he said ; "you're
the Eppie that makes such nice scones !"

Eppie laughed. "Ay, I'm her !" she
made answer, "and ye 'll taste my scones
to your tea."

"Thank you," said the boy. Then he
took hold of the hand of his little brother,
who had not spoken. "This is Willie ;
and I 'm Roy, after Uncle, you know."

Willie held out his hand, and Eppie
shook it gravely. Then the minister
struck in. "That'll do for an introduction,"
he said. "Take the lads up to their room
now, Eppie, and have them wash their
faces : they are black with train smoke."

The twins glanced at Mr. McAllister
reproachfully ; their feelings were hurt.
But Eppie was not aware of it. She led
the way to the south room where the boys
were to sleep, talking of trains and the
dirtiness of travelling, and of the one long

trip of her life, when she went "a' the way to Glaskie." The children were silent. Their spirits sank in the loneliness of the old gray house, buried among the moors. From their windows in England they could see an exciting view of busy streets, of horses and men ; of stirring, hurrying life. Here all the view was of rolling, heather-grown slopes, with no sign of life but a few cows in the distance. And, worst of all, mother was not here !

"I don't like the Manse ; I wish we were in England again," said Willie to Roy, as they lay awake in the big, strange bed that evening.

Roy broke into a storm of sobs.

"I wish I could go to mother !" he cried passionately. "I wish I had n't got to be anywhere ! I wish I was n't alive ! What 's the good of being alive now mother's gone ? "

Willie was sobbing, too, but softly and hopelessly.

"We've *got* to stay," he managed to repeat through his tears.

"I *won't* stay!"

"Yes you will; you've got to!"

Willie never gave up a point, and Roy, used to arguing with him by the half-hour, was not irritated by his obstinacy now. On the contrary, the prospect of an argument diverted his mind. He drew the sleeve of his night-shirt across his eyes and sat up in bed.

"Now you just listen to me! We can run away as easily as anything. We'll watch for the coach, and when we hear it in the distance, we'll slip out of the side door and go down the road a bit—out of sight of the house—and wait—— "

"They'd see us," interrupted his brother.

"No they wouldn't! And when the coach comes *quite* close, we'll jump out of the bushes and call, ' Hi! stop!' and that funny man who gave us the pepper-

mints, will help us up in front, and then "—
Roy came to a pause abruptly, for a figure
stood at the door. It was Eppie, carrying something on a plate. She came
towards them and peered through the
dusk into the two little white, tear-stained
faces.

"Ye 're not sleepin' yet ? Ay, I thought
as much ! An' greetin' [crying], the two
of ye ! That 's a poor beginning : it winna
do, lads, it winna do ! " She put her
warm, kind arms round the boys, and
drew the two curly heads down against
her merino bodice ; and this time they did
not pull away from the embrace, but
leaned gratefully on that friendly bosom
and cried.

"Ye dinna look to see what I brought
ye," she said in her low, soft voice, in a
few minutes. Her accent, though not so
refined, reminded Roy and Willie of their
mother's. It made them feel at home
with Eppie.

They now strained their eyes to see
what it was that lay on the plate.

The summer twilight had faded almost
into darkness, but they could dimly make
out a pile of oval, delicious-looking cakes.

" They're short-cake," said Eppie, "an'
just bakit; take them an' eat them an'
then go to sleep. Ye'll feel mair heart-
some in the morn."

The boys cuddled down in bed with the
plate of short-cakes between them, and
munched silently. The cakes were very
good. When the last crumb was gone,
they put the plate on the floor, and were
in dreamland before one could have
counted fifty, for they were tired out with
their long journey and with crying.

At an unearthly hour (as they thought)
the next morning, Eppie waked them up,
and bade them be quick and dress themselves and come down-stairs to prayers.
She had a severe, business-like manner to-
day, and no one would have imagined that

she was the kind of person to creep into the room after one had gone to bed, bringing one short-cake.

"I don't like Eppie so much this morn-ning, do you?" Roy whispered to Willie, as they went in to breakfast, after the minister had read a psalm and some prayers.

"No," replied his brother. "She's got a sort of look as if she was sorry she was so nice to us last night."

Their uncle was very silent at the table, and Eppie, stern and red-faced from stoop-ing over the kitchen fire, came and went about the room, without taking the least notice of them. The boys hated oat-meal, but it seemed to be all the breakfast they were to have at the Manse. Oat-meal and new milk, which was given them in bowls of generous size. They had been taught that most valuable lesson— never to ask for anything not on the table; and to take what was offered without making a fuss if it did not happen to suit them ; but it was evident that the porridge and milk were not what they were used to eating ; and Mr. McAllister remarked in an abstract manner as they rose, leaving their portion half finished, that simple fare was the rule in his house, and nothing else was fit and wholesome for young folk.

The boys blushed and hung their heads at this hidden rebuke, which they felt they hardly deserved. They looked at their uncle with a sense of dread ; he was not the man they had always thought of as their dear Uncle Robert, the loving brother their mother had told them about. This was a terribly exacting, grim kind of an Uncle Robert : they felt as if he had never been a boy himself. But he had taken them into the study, and seated himself at the table with the brown cloth, not asking them to sit, but letting them stand before the table as if it was a Bar of Justice, and he the Judge.

" We will now see what you know about English History," he announced.

The twins held their heads higher. They had been well taught, and Uncle Robert should see it. In fact, he did. He was surprised at the amount of what his little nephews had read, and still more at the thoroughness of their knowledge ; but being of the old-fashioned opinion that praise was harmful, he gave none ; going on with his questions in a harsh, cold voice, as if he suspected the boys of trying to take him in in some way. After English History, came Arithmetic ; then Geography ; then Grammar. Last of all Mr. McAllister requested them to write a page at his dictation. They came out with a brilliant record, and a wiser person would have told them that their honest efforts were very creditable to them, and that, having started in so good a manner, it the more behoved them to go on working well, and pleasing those set over their

education.   Instead, the minister merely
said in an unenthusiastic way : " That will
do for this time ; you need not study any
lessons to-day, as it is the first day.   I
will set you some for to-morrow.   You
may run out of doors now and play—only
mind and be in at the minute to dinner."

The twins went out, not running, as
their uncle had said they could, but walking slowly and seriously, with grave faces.

They went down the garden-path, and
across the white, dusty road, and up the
moor opposite, for a little way, and then
sat down ;—all without taking counsel together, for they were almost always of
one mind about what they wanted to do.

Roy spoke first.   His face was flushed,
and his lip trembled.

" I can't bear Uncle Robert !"

" And I can't."

" He is just a—a—what's the name of
that awfully wicked Roman Emperor that
killed all those nice people ?"

7

" Nero ? " suggested Willie.

" Yes, Nero, the tyrant.   Uncle Robert
is a *tyrant*.   He wanted to frighten us
and make us make mistakes in the things
he asked us about, so that he could find
fault with us.   He is perfectly horrid !
I don't see how mother could have had
such a horrid brother."

Willie considered the matter.

" *She* thought he was kind and nice ;
she always said so."

" That was just because she was kind
and dear and lovely and an angel, herself," said Roy with a shaking voice.
" mother always thought well of people,
even if every one else knew they were
hateful."

Willie was silent for a while.   At length
he said gently,

" Don't you s 'pose we ought to try and
do it too ? "

" Do what too ? "

Roy had drifted away from the subject

in hand, a characteristic thing with him.
Willie never left a train of thought half-
worked out.

"I meant, ought n't we to try to think
well of everyone, as mother did. I'm
sure she would *want* us to, Roy."

Roy looked uncomfortable.

"And it is the most sensible thing,
too," Willie went on, "for we have to be
with people, whether we like them or not;
and it's more disagreeable to be with
them if we hate them than if we are fond
of them."

Willie's first reason for charitable judgment was better than his last, but his
brother was not disposed to yield to
either at the moment.

"Of course *mother* could feel kindly to
anyone," he said impatiently, "but we are
not good, like her."

"We could be if we tried," said Willie
dogmatically.

"Besides," Roy went on, "even she

would allow that Uncle Robert was unkind this morning."

"I think he does n't remember how he used to feel when *he* was a boy," suggested the other. "Maybe we 'll be just the same when we 're as old as he is. He must be awfully old—as old as forty, I should say!"

Roy laughed a boy's gay laugh; the idea of Uncle Robert's great age as contrasted with their nine years, amused him. Perhaps Willie was right,—he was often right, and age was the cause of their uncle's unattractive ways. And if this were so, of course, they could do nothing but bear with him; for "mother" had impressed on the twins that old people had a sort of sacredness about them, and were always to be listened to, and said "yes" to, and waited upon, and, above all,—*never* to be contradicted. He sighed, thinking all these things over. He almost wished that Uncle Robert had been young

enough to argue with, and—if matters
grew worse—to defy!

"I am really afraid you're right, Willie," he said thoughtfully, "and in that
case we can't do anything—except run
away!" he added with a bright recollec-
tion of the plan he had been explain-
ing the night previous, before Eppie
came in with the delicious diversion of
cakes.

Willie was not so ready as before to
oppose this scheme. He had conscien-
tiously tried to cheer Roy's mind, but
deep down in his own lay a discontent
and a rebellion as sincere as his brother's,
and he feared that he could not always
stay at Kirk-Andrew himself, bold as he
had seemed.

"We'll have to stop here a little while,
anyway," he answered rather faintly.
"We'll be bigger by and by, and then we
can go where we like."

Roy gave a snort.

" Bigger by and by ! " he repeated scornfully.   " If we wait till then——"

Willie was silent.

" And if we run away while we are little,
we have ever so much more chance of being taken as cabin-boys ; they don't want
big cabin-boys."

"Oh ! " said Willie.   There was one
thing that Roy had not thought of in this
cabin-boy scheme ; he had better point it
out before they went further with it.   Only
one boy was wanted at a time on a boat,
surely.

" Don't you think we had better be
something else, Roy ? " he said ; " because,
if we were cabin-boys,—why, we 'd be
separated, don't you see ? "

Roy's face fell.   He had certainly forgotten that.   To be separated was not to
be thought of for an instant.   Willie
thereupon suggested that they wait a year,
and after that, try for a place together on
a " man-of-war " as cook and steward ; or,

if possible, as first and second mate. This led to a deeply interesting discussion, which kept them so busily occupied that dinner-time—the oddly early dinner-time of Kirk-Andrew—took them unprepared ; for which their uncle reproved them.

"I told you not to be late, lads," he said in a voice colder than he knew. " I am never late for any of the occasions of life, myself. Time is a gift ; it must not be lightly wasted."

Roy looked at him earnestly. " I suppose you did n't care about not wasting time when you were young, did you, Uncle ? " he asked.

Mr. McAllister colored. "That is a disrespectful manner of speech," he said very sternly.

Roy's big brown eyes grew bigger ; he had not meant to be rude : he was only inquisitive.

"I beg your pardon," he said, "but Willie and I think you don't just remember how a boy feels, because you have been old so long, that 's all."

"Guide us!" murmured Eppie, who had that moment come in with a new dish. .

" And so we're going to try and feel a little older; and maybe you could try and feel a little younger, and so we should get along better," added Willie calmly.

The minister stared at them. Was this impertinence? The twins stared back.

A dull flush rose in the minister's cheeks. Then he spoke:

"I will be glad if you will eat, and not talk foolishly," he said. " The table is not the place for talking; especially for children."

So their well-meant effort at coming to an understanding with their uncle failed. Sorrowfully, and perhaps a little angrily, the boys ate their plain but wholesome meal, and a deeper gloom settled over their minds.

"The only thing is to run away," Roy announced when they had wandered out again. So they planned how it should be, sitting together on the wild moor-side, deaf to the lonely, sad cry of the curlew and the hum of the bees over the beautiful purple heather-bloom and the golden gorse, blind to the loveliness of the blue summer sky, and the wealth of splendid color all about them.

Willie did not take the opposite side, after his usual mode; he was convinced that Roy and Uncle Robert would never be able to live in the same house, and he would not stay where Roy could not. The hearts of the boys were hot with resentment at their mother's brother; the unloving brother who never spoke of her, and who seemed to care nothing for the children she had loved so well. Poor Mr. McAllister! It would have grieved him much if he had known how "Annie's lads" felt towards him. At the very time when

Roy and Willie were planning to run away from his house he was sitting in his study thinking of them and trying to understand what their words at dinner had meant.

"Old, am I?" he said to himself. "Like enough—though I did not know it! It needs young eyes to see that one has grown old: one is not ready to see it of one's self. Well, may be the lads have the right of the matter, and I have forgotten how I felt when I was a lad. I mind I got many a scolding for one ploy or another." He smiled to himself, the memories of boyhood beginning to flow in upon him. He had been rather a mischievous boy, as he realized now. Perhaps he had spoken a little sharply to the twins; he would be more patient in future. They were fine lads, bonny lads, with their mother's wide, honest gaze that feared nothing. A little time was needed to accustom them to the new life; he ought to

keep that in view.   And then he took up
a learned book on the Children of Israel
and forgot the children at the Manse.

Sunday came round, and the boys were
made aware that this was a different kind
of Sunday from the one they were used to
in England.

That was a very pleasant kind, and
they had always looked forward to it.
To begin with, they had more of mother
then than was possible on week-days.
Mother never seemed hurried on Sunday,
and everything disturbing was banished.
Troublesome matters were never talked
over on Sunday ; naughtinesses were only
punished by a gentle look of mother's
sweet eyes, which generally brought the
offender to her feet, penitent.

There was an indescribable air of peace
about mother's best dress—soft silk, with
a hushed, unobtrusive rustle to it ; the
boys had liked to sit on a footstool beside
her and lean their heads against its folds.

They had always had some delightful
book put by for Sunday, and in the morning
they had gone to the pretty little ivy-cov-
ered church, each holding one of mother's
hands; and in the afternoon, they had
taken mother for a walk, and led her up the
fields outside the town, to find wild flowers.
Then after tea, they had all three drawn
around the piano, and mother had sung for
them out of the hymn-book till bedtime.

Sunday at Kirk-Andrew was a different
affair.   An atmosphere of gravity was
everywhere.   The minister looked so serious that the twins wondered if he felt
ill.   Eppie refused to smile when they
bade her a good morning.   Breakfast
passed in awful silence, and, immediately
after, they were told to get ready for
"kirk."   The service did not begin for a
long time yet; so they were at a loss to
know why it was necessary to get ready thus
early.   They asked Eppie, and she told
them that what was meant by "getting

ready" was sitting still, reading their books, and not running wild over all creation, as they did on other days.

The twins accordingly seated themselves demurely in the doorway, each with a book. The minister, passing a few minutes after, asked with an air of suspicion, "what they were reading?" The boys held up two brightly bound volumes.

"*Travels in Central Africa*" exclaimed their uncle in a tone of horror, "What like book is this for the Sabbath?"

Roy, to whom the work belonged, blushed angrily.

"Mother always let us read travels on Sunday," he said defiantly, "and these are splendid. There's an account of a perfectly delightful missionary who used to hunt lions, and the lions nearly ate him up once, only he just got his gun in time, and—"

"That will do," said Mr. McAllister, holding up his hand. "It may be a good enough book for a week-day, but here you must read only grave books on the Sabbath." He took both volumes from the boys and bore them into the house. In a little while he brought out two severe-looking " memoirs," and laid them in their laps in silence. Roy waited until his back was turned, and then hurled his into the wet grass.

"The hateful man!" he said through his teeth. Willie went and picked up the " memoir" and put it down on the step; for which Roy scowled at him.

" I wanted him to see it there; it serves him right," he said.

" It's just as well not to make him any crosser than he is."

" We are n't obliged to read his horrid old things. As if mother did not know what was proper for us!"

"It is just as well not to vex him, though," rejoined Willie.

It was a relief to be called to come to

'kirk.' It seemed a very small and bare kirk, quite unlike any church they had ever seen before.

The pews were like little cattle-pens, except for a table in the centre, with a black cloth over it. The clerk gave out the key-note of the long metrical psalms on a tuning-fork; and the twins learned, to their great surprise, that in kirk, people stood up to pray and sat down to sing. They could not remember this, and were constantly doing the wrong thing, which confused them much.

They were shocked to see old women and girls eating candy, and chewing green herbs. It shocked them, too, at first, to see so many dogs in church; but as the long, uncheerful service went on, they were grateful for their presence, and began to think which ones they would each like to have for their own. By the time Mr. McAllister stood up to preach, Willie had become very sleepy, and his uncle gave him a reproving look from the pulpit which he did not see.

The sermon was long and learned, and quite beyond the boys' understanding; and,—sad to say,—they were both asleep before it ended. Now, in the old days in England, when they had felt sleepy in church, it had been their pleasant privilege to put their heads against mother, and softly float away into dreamland. Therefore, Eppie sitting close to him in the Manse pew—it befell that Willie, growing drowsy, dropped his yellow head on her plump arm. But Eppie shook him, and set him in his place again. Two minutes after, he did the same thing—and so did she. But when he fell against her for the third time, she let him stay. And, presently, Roy's brown curls were resting on her other arm; and she sat so through the remainder of the service, her cheeks scarlet, staring defiantly past the gaping faces of the congregation.

"The poor wee things!" she was say-ing to herself, "they canna help it! they're fair silly wi' sleep; an' it's little they would know if they were keepit awake by pinchin' an' shakin.'"

But the minister took another view, and when the Manse dinner was ready, the boys were not allowed to come to table, nor to partake of the very nice pudding Eppie had made specially for them. And this seemed to Eppie a terrible punish-ment. She was angry with her master, and, as was sometimes the case, told him so in her own fashion; slamming the door when she went through; putting the dishes down upon the board violently, and sniffing disdainfully. The minister did not know what was wrong, and waited for enlightenment.

But when the enlightenment came, it was in a way he had not expected.

The twins sat together on the big bed that evening and Roy spoke:

"It will be a moonlight night: that's just what we wanted, is n't it?"

"Just.　When shall we start?"

"Not until they have shut up the house and gone to sleep."

"And what shall we do first?"　Willie always gave Roy the lead.

"We will go across the moors till we get to the sea. You know, Eppie says the sea is that way—" he pointed out of the window by the bed.

Willie looked a little anxious.

"You are sure you don't want to go and hide by the road, and wait for the stage, and get the peppermint-man to take us,—the way we meant to do before?"

"No," said Roy decidedly. "I've thought that over and I see it would n't do. He would not take us; he'd tell Uncle, and Uncle would shut us up on bread and water for months, maybe."

"I suppose he might," Willie admitted, sadly, "but the sea is so awfully far off, Roy; and we don't really know the way a bit."

"If you're *afraid*—" began his brother scornfully.

"I'm not afraid, only—— "

"Then don't take all the fun out of everything!"

"Only, if we got lost, Uncle Robert would find us, maybe, and nothing *could* be worse than *that*, could it?"

"Nothing!" agreed Roy with a shiver. "But we will never, never be found! We will disappear like—like——"

"Like anything!" suggested Willie, and Roy assented.

"I fancy he'll feel rather bad when he discovers our flight," said Roy; "he'll be glad we're gone, but he will have a dreadfully bad conscience about having made us do it. At least, I hope so!"

And with this, the twins rose and fell to completing their preparations for the journey. These took a good while, and still there were two hours to wait before the house would be quiet enough to make it safe to start. They laid themselves down on the bed, and then, very naturally, they dropped asleep.

Roy woke with a shiver. The moonlight was streaming into the room, and a bright ray streaked Willie's golden hair, making it look like silver. He sat up and looked about him, wondering what was the matter, that he and his brother should be lying on the outside of their bed with all their clothes on. Then he remembered.

"Willie!" he cried in a loud whisper, "Willie! wake up!"

"What is it?" asked the boy drowsily.

"Why, we have been asleep, and we had no business to be!" Roy said. "We have lost a lot of time, and we must n't lose another minute. Wake up, I say!" He shook Willie briskly as he spoke, and dragged him into a sitting posture. Willie rubbed his eyes and yawned and presently realized everything. But it seemed as if sleep had cooled his eagerness.

"Oh, Roy—I say, suppose we give it up; just for to-night, anyway!"

"Give it up! Why, you precious little duffer!" Roy stood in the middle of the

floor gazing at him in surprise and contempt.

Willie colored under the look.   But
he was not wholly subdued by it.

"It's so cold; and so awfully dark!
Why don't we go to-morrow morning when
we can see where we are going?"

Roy made no verbal reply, but went to
his box, took out a small purse, and put it
in his pocket.

"I think I have all the things I want,
now," he said.   Willie understood that
appeal was useless, and obediently prepared to follow him.

"Of course you need not come if you
don't want to," remarked Roy in a chilly
tone.   "Stay, by all means, if you like
Uncle Robert better than me." The result
of this speech was that Willie flung his
arms about Roy, and then Roy embraced
Willie; for it was terrible to the twins to
quarrel; and then they softly opened their
door, and softly crept down the dark

stairs, and, after a slight struggle with the
hall window, were out - of - doors. The
moonlight was so brilliant that it showed
every tree and bush, and every high gray
rock on the moor opposite. The shadows
it cast were proportionately black and
deep; and the more sensitive Willie
shivered as he looked. But for arousing
Roy's scorn afresh, he would have returned
to the Manse and waited for day. As it
was, he drew a long breath and went forward. They crossed the white high road
and began the ascent of the moor. It
sloped upward about two hundred feet,
and then dropped somewhat abruptly into
a little valley, beyond which it rose again
more steeply. The boys began to realize
that there was a good deal more of it than
they had seen from the Manse. They
walked on and on, always getting higher
in spite of the little valleys. At last they
came to a piece of swampy ground where
the hard, heather-grown soil gave place to

soft moss,—moss such as they had never
seen before ; moss which showed, even in
the moonlight, rich hues of crimson, and
which felt like a thick rug to their feet.
They got those same feet very wet in
crossing this place, and were not sorry to
regain the solid ground, for, as Willie said,
" It might have been a bog and swallowed
them up."

The way grew steeper and steeper, the
air colder, as they went on.   The boys'
clothing was soaked with dew, and their
feet grew weary with hard climbing.   After
a time they sat down to rest under a rock.
If Roy had begun to wish that he had
waited for day, he would not allow as
much.

Willie loyally kept silent.   And, as the
weird stillness around them was soothing,
they presently dropped into a dull slumber,
leaning back against the boulder.   The
sun was just rising in a tangle of mists as
they opened their eyes once more.   They

felt very cold, and, when they tried to rise up, very stiff and cramped.

"Oh, how queer my arms and legs do feel!" cried Willie, twisting and turning himself about.

"I fancy we ought n't to have gone to sleep out-of-doors," answered Roy. "We have caught cold, and that's a nuisance for you, old man, because your colds always last such a long time. Let's eat the short-cakes now; they'll be all the break-fast we will get, most likely."

Eppie, (kind, unconscious Eppie) had brought two cakes up to the boys the evening before, in consideration of their abbreviated dinner. The cakes tasted particularly good as the hungry children ate them out under the sky; and each hid from the other a coward-longing to be in the warm Manse kitchen, with more short-cakes to come: such weakness was not to be confessed. Roy brushed the crumbs from his mouth and got on his feet.

"We must be pushing on," he said in a brisk tone. Then he remembered that this was a new day, and a day full of new difficulties and dangers.

"We must say our prayers, Willie."

Then they began their climb again, up and up, the tawny bracken and purple heather and wet grass under foot, and the endless moor always beyond.

"I wish the sea wasn't so far off," poor Willie gasped by and by.

"Oh, we'll get there some time," Roy gasped back.

"To-night, do you suppose?"

"Well, perhaps. But not if we give out at the start."

"At the start!" Willie cried. "Why, Roy, we've been walking and *walking*, and I hoped we were getting nearly there."

"It does n't do to be impatient," Roy made answer sagely. "We knew we should have a bad time getting away, and

we must be plucky and keep up each
other's hearts—not fuss."

Willie was hurt ; he had tried with all
his might to be plucky and cheery, and
Roy never appreciated his efforts! But
he toiled on.

And now came a new difficulty such as
they had not reckoned upon. They had
reached the top of a very high ridge,
when they were aware that the sky was
overcast, and that a fine, misty rain was
beginning to fall. They pushed on, but
the mist pushed on faster. In five
minutes, they could not see two feet
before them.

" We must wait till this is over," Roy
said carelessly. So they drew under the
edge of a boulder again, and waited.
But time passed, and the mist only grew
more dense. The boys chafed at the
waste of time; they did not know that a
great danger was over them. To be lost
in a real mountain mist is what the oldest

mountaineer dreads. Their clothing was now wet through and through, and their teeth chattered.

After a while Roy heard Willie sobbing softly to himself. He put an arm about him tenderly.

"Don't, *please!*" he begged. Willie caught him in a tight hug.

"I did n't mean to, Roy, truly, but I 'm afraid! Yes, I am! I wish we were back at the Manse. You must not be angry ; I can't help it!"

"I 'm not a bit angry." If Roy had told what was in his heart, he, too, longed to be at the Manse. He saw what a mad thing it had been,—this running away. But he was too proud to allow it. Besides, he had led his brother into it, and he must keep calm and brave, whatever came.

He held Willie closer. What if this chill and fright should make him ill? Willie had always been the delicate one— the one mother had worried about. Suppose Willie were to die out here, in this awful fog, away from any help? He could have screamed with agony. Instead, he said in a very quiet voice,——

"I think maybe the sun will come out pretty soon. Don't fret: I'm here, Willie; I'll take care of you!"

When Eppie called at the boys' door— "Time ye wakened!" and got no answer, that Monday morning, she opened the door, and went into the room.

In a moment, she saw what had happened. And "to make assurance doubly sure," here was a scrap of ruled paper on the table, saying:

"dear epie This is to tell you we have run away because uncle robert is to hard To please. we think you are nice and we will see you again some day. yours with love, Roy and Wilie."

Eppie carried the scrap to the minister's door.

"Noo ye see what ye hae done," she cried ; "read that !"

Mr. McAllister took the paper and stared at it blankly.

"What does this mean ?" he asked with a pale face, his hand shaking.

"What does it mean ?" repeated Eppie fiercely. "It means ye hae driven the poor bairns to run fro' ye, wi' your harryin' them this way and that way—What else ? Keepin' them in their bed-chamber a' Sabbath because they sleepit a bit in kirk, an' no givin' them enough to eat, the poor wee laddies ! Think shame to yersel', Minister !"

Mr. McAllister looked at Eppie in amazed silence ; never had she so addressed him before.

"I will allow no such talk as this, my woman," he said sternly, "but if ye have any sense in your head, tell me if the lads had said aught to show they had an idea of this beforehand."

"I dinna ken," Eppie replied, a little subdued; "I canna mind—unless it would be Roy askin' me was the sea very far fro' this? An' anither time, Willie telled me he would like fine to be a sailor, an' maybe it would be a sailor he was to be, some day. I'm thinkin' the lads hae gone over the moor to find the sea."

"I will set some folk to seeking them," said the minister; and he went out, not staying for breakfast. Eppie sank down on the stairs crying.

The minister went to the small cottage of "Lang" Jock Mackenzie, the shepherd. Jock listened to his tale without a change of feature, only taking a pinch of snuff, and saying gravely, "Ay, that might be;" for he was a cautious man. But when Mr. McAllister asked if he were willing to go out and try to find the boys, he said at once that he would go, and that his collie, Meg, should go too.

"Meg's a powerfu' fine nose for a scent,"

he added. "I will be steppin' tae the Manse, an' Eppie will be givin' me a bit o' the bairns' clothes, an' Meg will find them, dinna fear."

After Lang Jock, the minister saw big Sandy Ford, and little Jamesie Campbell, and two or three more; and when they had made their plans, they separated, each taking a different way.

Lang Jock and his faithful dog chose the moor opposite the Manse, and when Meg had carefully sniffed at the jacket Eppie had given to the shepherd, she gave an impatient bark, as if to say— "Well, let us get to work!"

"Gae find the lads, Meg!" cried Jock, "Gae find!" and she laid her sharp, slender nose to the ground, and disappeared into the mist, which was still over everything, though gradually thinning.

Jock followed, calling to the dog from time to time. After a long absence, back she came, and jumped up, whining, and

trying to tell him to hurry. And hurry
he did, striding up and down the ridges,
till he came to a big boulder, and as Meg
rushed to it and back again, barking
wildly, stooped and found two unconscious little figures, lying wrapped in one
another's arms!

Roy waked from a long sleep to hear a
sound of short, hard breathing close to
him. He turned slightly and saw a man's
figure stooping over at the side of his bed,
its shoulders heaving. Rather queer that,
he thought; but no queerer than his being
in bed. Where ought he to be? He
tried to remember. Why, yes—he had no
business to be in bed; he was on the
moor with Willie, and it was high time
they were going on now, because the mist
had all gone and the sun was shining.
Or, was it a lamp? He couldn't tell.
Funny to have a lamp out on the moor!
Only everything seemed to have grown

9

funny.   And why did n't Willie say something?   That was the queerest thing of
all!   Where *was* Willie, anyway?   He
tried to see around the room ; he called
in a faint voice, " Willie ! "

  The figure at the bedside came close
and peered anxiously into his face.   It was
his uncle !

  Roy looked up at him, and held out a
wavering little hand.

  " Uncle Robert," he said weakly, " I
suppose you are going to put us on bread
and water, but I want you to let Willie
off the easiest ; he would never have run
away but for me.   I made him."

  Mr. McAllister strode to the window
and blew his nose.   Then he came back.

  " Eh, my lad," he said wistfully, " What
made you run away from me ? "

  " We thought you did n't like us, and
we meant to be sailors," was the simple
answer.   " Please,—where is Willie ? " he
went on eagerly.

"Ah, Willie is a sick lad," said the minister sadly. "It's he who will be the most likely to remember this foolish piece of work. Roy, man, he is too ill to see you—too ill to leave his bed in the other room there for a long while, I'm afraid. And to think I should have frightened my own Annie's lads so that they ran from my house!"

Roy opened his eyes wide, for, if he could believe them, stern Uncle Robert— harsh Uncle Robert—was crying!

He had sat down again close by the bed, and now Roy stretched out his hand once more and touched the minister's.

"Please don't, Uncle!" he sobbed. "I'll never run away again—and when Willie gets well, we won't go to sleep in church, or do *anything* any more!"

And then the queerest thing of all happened, (as Roy told Willie by and by), for Uncle Robert actually leaned over and kissed him!

"God has taught me a lesson," he said humbly.

And the twins stayed at the Manse, and grew to love it. And, so far as I know, they are not and never will be, sailors.

AUL MAY was a pale-faced, large-eyed boy of seven, very unlike the strong, red-cheeked troop of cousins with whom he had come down for a holiday in Cornwall. He was unlike them in his ways, too, for he was as quiet and shy as they were noisy and bold. And so it happened that while they romped and built sand-castles, Paul would wander off along the shore by himself.

He was never dull, for he had a bright mind under his brown curls, and quick, clear eyes which noticed everything about them.

He had loved to go to the big museums in London, and see the fine collec-

tions of minerals and shells there, and
now he was planning to have a museum
of his own.   He begged an old tin box
from his aunt, and took it with him on his
walks, stopping every now and then to
put in a new treasure.   The latest thing
he had found was a hermit-crab.   Did you
ever see one?   It is not a very nice-look-
ing creature.   It eats up some kinds of
shell-fish, and then lives in the empty
shell; and you are surprised to pick up a
big, spiral whelk-shell, and find crab's
claws coming out of it!

Paul was much pleased with his "find,"
but he was not sure about putting it into
the tin box, because it was alive.   He sat
down on a bit of gray rock to think it
over, and then, for the first time, he became aware that he was very, very hungry.   Also, that he was a long way from
home.

He gazed around him, and saw that this
part of the beach was new to him.   Walk-

ing on and on, with the tender touch of
the warm wind on his cheek, and the lull-
ing plash of the green baby-waves in his
ear, his eyes bent on the sand,—he had
not noticed how far he was straying.
Now, he began to look serious—first, because it is never pleasant to feel hungry
when no food is to be had ; and secondly,
because he was very tired. And thirdly,
because his Uncle May was very strict
about coming late to meals, and might not
let him have any dinner when he got
home.

Paul grew more and more sober, and
he was so much absorbed in his own
thoughts that he did not see that he was
no longer alone on the wide reach of
shore. An elderly gentleman, dressed in
an old-fashioned black suit, was standing
at a little distance, leaning on a gold-
headed cane, and watching the boy with a
smile on his lips.

Paul's musings ended in a conviction

that the sooner he set out on his home-
ward way, the better, and he rose up to
go,—and saw the old gentleman smiling
at him.

Paul was generally shy of strangers, but
he liked this particular stranger's face,
with its kind gray eyes, so he went up
to him without more delay, and asked,
" Please—can you tell me the time ? "

" The time," said his new acquaintance,
drawing from the pocket of his silk waistcoat a thick gold watch with a bunch of
seals hanging from it, "the time, little
boy, is ten minutes of two."

Paul's face grew so long at this, that the
owner of the watch asked in his turn,——

"What time would you like it to be ? "

"One o'clock," replied Paul instantly.

" Luncheon-time, eh ? " said the old
gentleman with a twinkle in his eye.

" Yes sir."

" And where do you come from, my
young traveller ? "

"From ' Beach House '—a long way off. At least, it must be a long way, though I did n't think so when I was walking."

"The way is apt to seem longer when we turn back," said the other. "But now, how will you manage? Can you get back to Beach House without having some refreshment first? Suppose—suppose now, little boy, that you come and lunch with me!"

Paul looked up at him in surprise.

"I mean it," said the old gentleman with a laugh which seemed to match his eyes. "Come now, are you not *very* late for luncheon at home?"

"Yes," murmured Paul, blushing.

"And won't you be scolded for that?"

"Yes," with a deeper blush.

"Perhaps not get much luncheon when the scolding is over, eh?"

Paul could not answer this question, but the old gentleman saw he had guessed aright.

"Well then, had you not better come
in and take 'pot-luck' with me?"

Paul did not know what "pot-luck"
was, but he felt very much inclined to
accept his new friend's invitation. Still he
hesitated.

"Ah! I see how it is!" cried the
stranger, "You are afraid that if you stay
away so long your mother will be anxious.
That's right, my boy, that's quite right!"

Paul suddenly burst into tears.

"My mother is dead! She died last
winter; and oh, I wish—I wish ——"

The old gentleman's silk waistcoat
seemed to have come close to the weeping
child, he did not know how; he could
only lean against it and sob. And then
he heard the old gentleman whispering
huskily,—

"There—I'm sorry I said it! Don't
cry, my dear, don't cry. Ah! me, it does-
n't feel like fifty years since *my* mother
died!"

He took out a large red silk handkerchief and wiped Paul's eyes gently.

" Then you 'll take luncheon with me ? " he said presently. " Your—your friends won't mind ? "

" Oh no, they won't miss me. I 'm out on the beach alone nearly all the time. Only, Uncle *is* very strict about not being *late !* "

" Very well, then," said the stranger. " We have not far to go, and directly after luncheon I 'll drive you over to Beach House."

Much cheered by this information, Paul put his small brown hand into the black-gloved hand of his companion, and trustfully followed him, away from the beach, up a few hundred yards of shady lane, and past some cottages, till they came to a large iron gate. Beyond the gate was an avenue, overarched by splendid trees, and the gentleman led Paul up the avenue and into the porch of a large house, so covered with vines that only a patch of its gray stone could be seen here and there through the green.

The porch opened into a lofty hall, with oak floor and walls and furniture ; and old pictures of ladies and gentlemen in queer costumes ; and stags' heads, and stuffed birds, and weapons, and armor,—but Paul could only get a passing glimpse of all these things, for the gentleman hurried him into a long, low-studded dining-room, where the big table was laid for one, and called to a man-servant, who looked as old as his master, "Another plate, William !"

That was a delightful luncheon. Between courses, Paul's host asked what he carried in his tin box ? And Paul opened it, and spread all the contents on the white table-cloth, and proudly confided to this friendly listener his plan of a private museum.

"Upon my word !" said the old gentleman ; and as Paul, growing enthusiastic,

explained the peculiar value of each speci-
men, he repeated the exclamation several
times very heartily. Paul was especially

proud of the hermit-crab, and talked about
it a great deal.

"To be sure—to be sure," said his
host, watching the eager child-face kindly.
Then he pulled out the big watch again,
and bade Paul finish his sweet omelette,

for it was nearly time for the carriage to come around.

They drove over to Beach House in a big yellow barouche drawn by a pair of grays, fat from little exercise and good feeding. As they rolled through the narrow streets, people came to their doors and looked after them, and said wonderingly—" There be Sir John Tremayne, but who 's the little lad ? "

Dr. May was very polite to his visitor, and when Sir John said at parting—" I hope you will let your nephew pay me another visit very shortly—" he said he should be most delighted, and thanked him for his kindness with every sign of gratitude and respect. And Paul was not scolded.

Paul paid a great many visits to Sir John in the next month. Every time he saw the old Baronet he seemed to love him more. Paul had grown to know the place quite well now. He liked to peep into the great drawing-room furnished in yellow brocade, whose stiff chairs and sofas repeated themselves over and over in the full-length mirrors around the walls. There was an old, old harpsichord, in one part of the room whose keys he had once ventured to touch, and whose voice sounded sweet though cracked—like that of an old singer. The shades of this room were always drawn down, and the half-light was mysterious. The air was fragrant with the scent of rose-leaves and spices from a big blue china "pot-pourri."

But Paul liked best the old-fashioned garden, a delicious wilderness of clove-pinks and sweet-peas, and I know not what else, with mossy fruit-trees standing up here and there, their old limbs bending under ripening fruit.

Bees haunted this garden and butterflies and dusky moths. It was a place of many delights.

But now all these joys were drawing to

an end, for the May family were going
back to London.

They were to leave on the sixth of September, and on the fifth, Paul went to bid
Sir John good-by.

The old house looked very peaceful in
the golden afternoon light. Bevis, the
aged mastiff, rose from the porch as he
saw the boy coming, and advanced toward
him, wagging his tail.   Paul put one arm
over the brown neck and they went on
to the house together.   Sir John met
them in the porch. He had meant to
seem very cheerful, but his eyes grew
moist as they took in the two figures.

" Well, my dear ! " he cried, " Come in !
Mrs. Burton is just carrying tea into the
blue parlor."

Mrs. Burton, the stout housekeeper, had
a soft spot in her heart for the little boy,
whom every one at the manor loved.

On this evening she had made him
one of her famous plum-cakes, and gar-

nished the table with moss-roses from the garden.

Sir John and his young guest made great efforts to laugh and talk as much as usual, but they did not succeed very well.

After tea, the old man laid his hand on the boy's shoulder and said:

"Come with me, I have something to show you."

He led Paul into a room which he had never seen before. It was rather small, panelled in white and gold, and had faded hangings of rose-colored satin.

Sir John shut the door softly.

"This was my mother's *boudoir*," he said.

Paul looked up into the old man's face with speaking eyes.

Sir John went forward and drew a silken veil from a picture on the wall.

It was the portrait of a young lady in a white frock fastened at the waist with a narrow rose-colored ribbon. She held in one slim hand three moss-roses like the ones from the manor garden. Her face was beautiful and smiling, and Paul thought her lively hazel eyes dwelt on him.

"That was my mother," said Sir John.

The little boy slipped his hand into the old man's fingers and pressed them silently.

"It was painted eighty-five years ago," Sir John went on dreamily, almost as if speaking to himself. "Eighty-five years ago. She was seventeen then, and when she was twenty—she died. Ah, yes! It's hard to be a motherless boy—hard—hard."

He was silent for a moment or two. Then he drew the veil over the portrait again, locked the door of the little room, and led Paul out into the open air. They passed across the velvet lawn, where no careless feet ever pressed the turf, and into the dear old flower-garden.

They were sitting there when the great clock struck six—warning them that the time to say "good-by" had come.

Paul stood up and began to pull off the paper wrappings of a little parcel.

It was nothing less than a bottle of sea water, at the bottom of which lay the hermit-crab.

"I—I thought—perhaps—you'd like it for a keepsake—after I'm gone," said Paul.

He had meant to speak quietly, but he choked on the last words, thrust the bottle into Sir John's hand, and flung himself down among the sweet-peas in a passion of tears.

When Paul was fast asleep that evening at Beach House, Sir John and Dr. May were holding a consultation together. The Baronet had made the doctor an offer,—namely, to take Paul for his own adopted son and heir, he being without a relative in all the wide world.

It took several hours to talk it all over, and arrange everything, but I may tell you that when the sixth of September came, Paul had tea with Sir John in the blue parlor again, very gayly this time. And Mrs. Burton's cake was better than before. And Bevis wagged his tail very hard, as if to say in his language: "Welcome, the heir of Sir John Tremayne!"

N the basement of a poor lodging-house over-looking a very poor street in a French seaport town, lived an old man called " M. Al-phonse." There must have been more of his name, but no one knew what the rest had been, and no one cared to know.

It might have been three years since M. Alphonse had moved into his cellar-room, and in all that time he had never had any visitors. But he was not quite alone, for he had to keep him company an old comrade who, like himself, had seen better days, and who now—like himself, bore patiently hard bedding and scanty food.

The old comrade was a lion.

He had once been young and strong and fierce, had shaken his shaggy mane, and opened his great jaws with a danger-

ous roar.   But that was a long time ago.
That was when M. Alphonse was a graceful young athlete, whose daring feats in
company with his " Unequalled African
Lion " had drawn great crowds in great
cities of the world.

In those days he was not called " M.
Alphonse," nor did he wear threadbare
clothes.   He wore cloth of silver ; and on
the circus-posters he was called — never
mind what !   It was all a long, long time
ago. So long ago it seemed to the feeble
old man, as he sat by his tiny charcoal fire
on winter evenings, that he almost wondered if it were a dream—all that life of
light and color and applause.

Now he was old and poor, and his
"African Lion " had grown old like himself.
Its fiery eyes were dim, and its limbs had
grown stiff.   Life had become sad to M.
Alphonse.

One day as he sat in his dark room, he
heard a childish voice call to him, and go-

ing to his door he saw the little daughter
of the concierge standing at the top of the
steps which led down into the basement.

"Good-day, mademoiselle," said M. Alphonse. "Did mademoiselle call?"

The little Aimée did not answer. Her
round blue eyes, growing used to the dim
light, had discovered the form of the lion
in its corner, and were fixed in terror upon
it.

"Ah! you are afraid of Leo!" said M.
Alphonse. "There is no cause, my little
one. He is too old and weary to move.
Besides, he is chained to the wall. He
cannot hurt you."

"But he is so big," faltered Aimée.

"He is very weak—and very gentle."

"Lions eat little girls," she said in a
whisper.

"Leo never did," M. Alphonse said with
a smile. "Besides, he has no teeth. Come
down and talk to me. I promise he shall
not touch you."

" I will talk to you," said Aimée, " but I will sit on the steps, near the top."

" Very well—then I will bring my chair and sit at the foot. What made you think of paying me a visit, little one ? "

" Because I thought you were lonely," she said simply. " I never saw you until yesterday when I met you coming in at the door. What makes you live here where it is so dark, M. Alphonse ? "

" I cannot afford a better room," said the old man. " Also, Leo can be with me here. If you were as lonely as I, little one, you would be glad of a companion."

Aimée glanced doubtfully at Leo.

" I should be afraid," she said. " But you do not mind the dark because you are like the curé. The curé says the good God sees in the dark and takes care of us."

M. Alphonse was silent. He did not know much about God's care.

" Yes, that is very good when one is frightened," the child went on. " Also, it is good to have some one come to see you. The next time I come I shall bring you a bag of bon-bons. My grandmother, every time I go to see her, gives me some. I love my grandmother much. Does any one love you, M. Alphonse?"

The old man sighed.

"I have had little love in my life," he said, "and all that there was ended long ago."

Aimée nodded her head sagely.

"That is very bad," she said.

"Once I had a little girl like you," the old man went on. "She loved me; but she is dead."

"That also," said the child. "Poor M. Alphonse!"

"Why did she die?" cried the man with a sudden fierceness, throwing out his arms as if to the child he had lost.

To his great surprise Aimée flew down the steps and flung her own small arms about his neck.

"I will love you like your little girl!"
she whispered, and he felt her warm tears
upon his cheek.   He held her close a
moment.

"But how can you love poor old Alphonse?" he said presently.

"Oh! I love all the world—except
Leo," said the child, suddenly remembering the dreaded form in the shadow.

"But if you love me, you must love
him, too," said Alphonse.   "Once he saved
my life when another wild beast tried to
kill me.   That was a long, long time ago.
I used to travel all over Europe with my
performing lions in those days."

"Tell me about it," pleaded the child,
settling herself comfortably on his knee,
her little white-capped head on his
shoulder.

"Ah, well! you see the three lions
were to jump through a great hoop.   Leo
first, Sara second, Nero last.   Now Nero
had a terrible hatred of me and he hated

the hoop. I called and cracked my whip. He growled and crouched. I called again. He laid his head flat upon his paws, lashed his tail and sprang, tearing my arm as I jumped aside. At that instant Leo sprang also—on the rebellious lion ; and as they rolled over, fighting, I made my escape from the cage. I have a scar on my arm still."

Aimée had clung tightly to Alphonse as he told his story. When he ended, she drew a deep breath.

" And you did not die ? "

" As you see."

" And Leo saved you ? "

" I have always said so."

She looked over the old man's shoulder at Leo.

" I think I love him a little," she said.

" He is my one friend," replied Alphonse. " We love each other, and we shall never be parted. As we have lived, we shall die, together."

Presently Aimée heard a voice some-where calling to her, and giving her new friend a kiss she slipped off his knee and went away up the steps.

" The next time, I will bring you some pink bon-bons," she said on the second step.

" Or white ones—which ? " she put this question seriously, turning around on the third.

" They are all delicious," said the old lion-tamer, smiling up at her from the gloom of the basement.

" For myself, I prefer chocolate," she added on the fourth step.

Her head had reached the top of the stairs now, and Alphonse could see the shining gold of her curls below the muslin cap.

He smiled still.

" Does Leo like chocolate ?"—this, from the head of the stairs.

" No, he likes nothing but meat."

"*Par exemple!*" cried the child in wonder.

She often came to see Alphonse after this. Sometimes it was to show the long blue stocking she was knitting, or to bring a large red apple or a small plum-cake.

But Alphonse wanted no present. It was her sweet face and her merry laugh and her soft little hands about his neck, of which he thought.

Winter was coming on, and the short days made the cellar-room darker than ever. It was cold and damp, too, and poor Leo shivered in his straw. Alphonse could do little work now, for his back was stiff and bent from rheumatism, so he earned very few francs. The tiny charcoal fire was tinier than ever, and sometimes the two old comrades had no food to eat.

But M. Alphonse never told Aimée this. When New Year's day came, she begged her father to ask her "dear old man in the cellar" to the family dinner-party.

At first Alphonse declared that he could not come — could not possibly come. But the little girl coaxed him into relenting.

"If you stay away—I—I also will stay away," she said with a pout.

"But no, most dear—" he said anxiously.

"As true as you live. I will not eat a mouthful."

"But, my Angel—"

"And there will be such *superb* things to eat !" she concluded, shaking her head.

M. Alphonse ventured no more refusals.

"If it must be—" he said meekly.

So he went.

At first the cheerful room of the concierge confused him with its light and brightness, and the half-dozen guests all chattering at once. The old man blushed for his poor clothes and ragged beard, and would not speak or look up.

But after the good dinner, where every one was kind to him, and Aimée sat by his side patting his hand, he felt more at his ease. A flash of the old fire came into his eyes. He even told one or two good stories which made the company laugh.

The good-natured concierge was pleased at his child's pleasure. Even Leo had a good meal sent down to him.

When Alphonse rose to go, they begged him to come again, and he made them a graceful bow, as he had used to do to an audience.

The winter went by. Warmer winds blew. Snow melted under the hot February sunshine.

One day Aimée came to her old man in the cellar with a bunch of violets and a bright face.

" Oh M. Alphonse—M. Alphonse! I am to make my First Communion! And at Easter! So soon! Art thou not glad?"

" Yes, dear little one. Thou wilt wear

a white dress, and a white veil on this little golden head; and thou wilt be all white—like the angels, Aimée, my well loved! I must see thee when thou art ready for church on Easter-day."

"But thou wilt be in the church too!"

"No."

"But yes! Always everyone is in church on the dear Easter-day. Didst thou never make a first communion, M. Alphonse?"

"Long, long ago," he said softly. His thoughts went back to a sunny morning in his native village, to a little gray stone church where the long beams of light slanting through the windows had fallen on rosy young faces and dazzling white garments. He was one of the children. He could smell the sweet country air full of flowers. He could hear the music.

Amiée laid her cheek against his. It was wet.

11

"Thou must come with me," she whispered.

" Perhaps," he whispered back.

That Easter was as bright a day as ever broke upon the world.

Even the basement room caught a little of its cloudless light.   Even the old lion stretched his stiffened limbs, turned his blind eyes towards the window, and snuffed the air which floated in as if scenting a new hope.

M. Alphonse was in a tremor.   He had not been able to decide whether or not to go to the church.   It was a long time since he had entered one.   He wanted to go— he dreaded to go.

As he was sitting with his head bent, by his little table, a flash of white came into the room,—Aimée, a vision of purity, carrying a tall spire of Easter lilies in each hand.

" Thou wilt come with me ? " she said. She put the lilies into a pitcher of water, and took the old man's hand, gazing up into his troubled face.

"Alas, little one! To be happy at Easter, one should be like thee!"

"Ah, but no, M. Alphonse, for I am very naughty sometimes. But if one is sorry, the Lord Christ comes and makes one good."

The tears came into her blue eyes.

Alphonse bent and kissed her suddenly.

"I will come," he said.

It all seemed like a dream as he walked through the crowded streets. It seemed like a dream to be in church again—to hear the great organ roll—to see the magnificent flowers—to hear the sacred words spoken.

He could see Aimée sitting among the other little girls,—a fluttering mass of snowy veils and frocks. His eyes never left her.

When all was over, she came to him outside and pulled him down to her.

" M. Alphonse," she whispered, "you look so—so glad. Did the Lord Christ come to you?"

The old man smiled and laid a hand on his breast.

" The Lord Christ is here," he said.

Aimée's father came up and touched his arm. "Can you find your way home alone, do you think, my friend?"

" My way? Oh yes—I am very near home," replied Alphonse. He looked up at the radiant sky, smiling.

The concierge felt a little anxious. The old man seemed as if scarcely conscious of what was going on about him.

" My little girl and I are going to the grandmother's"; said the concierge. "You are sure you can go home alone?"

Alphonse smiled the same tender, far-away smile.

" I am going home now," he said, and he turned away.

Early next morning the concierge went

himself to the basement room.   He felt anxious about the old man, and wanted to see how he had borne the fatigues of the day before.

All was very still.   The scent of the Easter lilies filled the darkness like incense.

" M. Alphonse ? " questioned the concierge.

There was no answer.

" M. Alphonse ? " He stepped to the low bed and touched the quiet form that rested there.

Then he started back.

The old lion-tamer lay sleeping the sleep no sound disturbs, and by his side, stretched at full length, lay the old lion.

They had died, as they had lived, together.

VIRGO, THE VIRGIN

 H E château of
Montarbre was a
gloomy-looking old
building, with nar-
row windows, and
immensely thick
walls. It had been built in times of war
and danger, when no one was safe unless
a good, strong barrier stood between him
and the world outside, and when air and
daylight were less important than shelter
from the enemy. It had survived the
fierce attack of armed peasants in the
days of the revolution, and had not suffered much from the slow destroyer, Time.
Its owners had always been men who
clung to the traditions of the past, and

who cared little for new ideas and new
ways. When any part of the château
needed repair, it was repaired on the old
plan ; and so, in the year 1895 it looked
from outside the same as it had in the
days of Henri Quatre. Even the old gardens were the same—stiff and stately, with
old-fashioned flowers, and dark, high
hedges ; no gay, giddy new-fangled blossoms or imported plants and shrubs. The
very servants looked as if they might have
been there a hundred years or so. There
was only one young thing about the
château, and that was the young heir,
Bertrand Philippe André de Lys, who
would some day be Lord of Montarbre.
The name suggested power and pride,
and conjured up a picture of a dashing
young noble, full of fire and spirit. But
Bertrand de Lys was not at all like that
picture. He was a frail little boy who
could not so much as walk, having been
an invalid since his fourth year.

At the time of this story he was four-
teen, and seemed at once older and
younger than his age : older, because his
face was grave and weary ; younger, because he was small and slight.   He lived
a very lonely life at the château, poor boy,
for he had no one near his own age to
talk to—no one at all but the servants
and the old priest who came to teach him.
The Marquis, his father, was in Paris,
and only came to Montarbre for a week's
visit now and then.   He sent Bertrand
books and games, and saw that he had
the best of attention, but as to staying in
the dull old place with his son—well,
really, no one could expect it of him, he
thought.   Bertrand's ill-health had been a
bitter sorrow to him, and he shrank from
being reminded that his son was an invalid for life.   It was his own distress of
which he chiefly thought ; and that was
much easier to bear in the city, where
there were so many things to distract and

amuse, than in the château beside the boy's couch.

Bertrand's sweet and beautiful mother had died when he was a baby, and he had never known her care, but his faithful nurse Nannette was with him, and her love was the warmest he had experienced.

He took it as a matter of course that his father should live at the family mansion in Paris, and that he had not much time to answer the formal, carefully-written letters which he wrote him every week, under the instructions of the curé. They were not very brilliant letters, for the boy had little to tell in his lonely and monotonous life.

The want he felt most keenly was that of young companions, and it was a grief to him that the village boys were not allowed to come inside the grounds. From his wheel-carriage on the broad terrace, he could see them, brown and sturdy, setting out on fishing trips, with their homemade rods of stripped branches and twine ; or carrying baskets for nuts and berries in the autumn; he could see how gaily they romped along the white, dusty road, pushing one another down just for the fun of it, wrestling and playing at fighting, all goodhumoredly, in the fullness of rude health. His sad blue eyes followed them as far as they could reach, and a sigh would come from his lips as they passed beyond his vision.

The little heir of Montarbre had been taught that it was the best thing in life to be born a noble, and not a poor peasant; but he would have given all the fine things he possessed to be a sunburned country lad, ragged and unlearned, if only like those he could run and jump and tussle, and play at fighting his mates. How gladly would he wear rough wooden sabots instead of the pretty buckled shoes that covered his idle feet! How happy it would be to come springing into the house after a five-mile tramp, hungry for bean-broth and coarse bread, instead of trying wearily to swallow the game and sauces of his clever cook !

He told these thoughts to the good old curé, and the curé sighed and stroked his thin little hand, and told him that it was not right to be discontented

" But how can I help it ? " asked poor Bertrand. " I should be less unhappy if I might have the village boys come here to see me, for then at least I could make them tell me about what they do, and that would be amusing ; but they are not allowed to come inside the grounds ! "

" M. le Marquis desires that, you know, my son."

" And I want to know why ? " demanded Bertrand rebelliously.

" Because the village boys are not suitable companions for the heir of Château Montarbre. They are rough, ignorant, and unpolished ; they say rude words ; they do not use correct grammar, and

their ideas are not the ideas of a person
in your class of life."

"Ah, bah!" Bertrand cried, throwing
out his hands with a gesture of contempt,
"I am tired of hearing what is proper for
my class of life! Me,—I wish I were the
child of a field-laborer, with rags to wear,
and onions and black bread to eat! Then
I could be happy! Then I need not be
always told—'M. Bertrand—that is un-
suitable to your rank!' or, 'M. Bertrand
—this or that will harm you!' I am so
tired—*so tired!*"

He finished his angry speech with a
pitiful sob, and the curé, who had been
about to reprove his pupil, took him in
his arms and said gently,—

"A great many things are hard to bear
now, but the time comes when we thank
those who seem severe while we do not
understand their motives. When you are
Marquis de Montarbre—"

Bertrand interrupted him.

"M. le Curé, there is a strange lady walking along the road!"

The curé looked. A lady, a stranger, was going past the château. She was simply but tastefully dressed, and she carried in her hand a large bouquet of wild flowers. As the man and the boy on the terrace watched her with interest, for strangers were not common in the village, she turned and called to some one, and then a little girl appeared round a turn in the road, and ran towards her.

"What a pretty little girl!" cried Bertrand; "I wonder who they are, and how they came here!"

"They are Americans," answered the priest, who now remembered hearing that a small villa half a mile away had been rented for the season. "They are at the house in the woods over there; I was told that the mother paints pictures from nature. They look like people of good standing—of culture."

"How I wish they would come in here and talk to me!" sighed Bertrand; "That little girl looks as if she could say amusing things! What sort of people are Americans?"

The curé perceived that the boy was taking too much interest in the strangers; it might be well to discourage this.

"Americans are dangerous people," he said gravely. "They have odd fancies in their heads: they call all men equals; they let every one do what he or she likes; their young children talk of politics, and their girls and boys are allowed to study and to play together. It is a very strange country."

Bertrand's pale cheeks had grown red with excitement, and his eyes flashed.

"A glorious country!" he cried; "When I am a man, I will go and live there!"

The curé looked at him in dismay.

"I think we will take up the study of

American history," he said. "It will show
you the dangers of liberty."

"As you will," replied the boy, smiling.
"But I warn you, M. le Curé, I am not
likely to be turned against a country such
as you have described. I love a country
where one may do as one likes, and where
all are equal. Vive l'Amerique!"

The curé went sadly away. Sometimes
he was afraid Bertrand had too strong a
will.

The study of American history was
delayed by an unlooked-for event. The
curé fell, the evening after his talk on
America, broke his leg, and was unable
to come to his pupil for some time.

Bertrand missed him much, and became
restless with nothing to do.

He saw the strange lady and her child
pass nearly every day, as he lay on the
terrace. They used to glance in at him,
and he liked their looks better and better.
It was too tantalizing to see them so far

off, and he suddenly made up his mind to
a bold course of action.

"Gervase," he said to the man-servant who wheeled his carriage about the
grounds, "this morning I wish to go out
on the road."

Gervase looked at him as if he did not
understand.

"On the road, Monsieur?"

"On the road—yes!"

"But, Monsieur—the directions of M.
le Marquis—"

"Will you obey me or not, Gervase?"
The man had never seen that flash in his
young master's eye before.

"But, certainly, Monsieur!"

"To the gates, then, and without delay!" For Bertrand wished to be in the
way when the American ladies passed,
and it was nearly their time for passing.
Gervase rolled the wheel-carriage down
the avenue, threw the gates open, and
took Bertrand out on the road.

"Which way, Monsieur?"

"To the woods!"

They had not been out more than ten minutes when Bertrand saw a bit of color above the bushes on the edge of the road. His heart began to beat hard; it was the wide pink muslin hat of the little girl.

In another minute she came into full view, stepping lightly along in advance of her mother, to whom she turned to speak. Her hands were full of flowers.

Now she saw the carriage. She looked up at her mother and seemed to say something concerning its occupant. As they drew nearer she walked more slowly, giving long glances at Bertrand, and again dropping her eyes. He, on his part, never took his own from her. She was the sweetest thing he had ever seen. He felt as if he could not let her pass by, the day would be so heavy afterwards. But he could not speak or stop her. His

strained face, so young and so suffering,
drew a look of kind sympathy from the
lady.   She read in it an appeal.

"Yes, I would, Ellie," she said softly to
her little daughter, as they came abreast
of the carriage.   But she did not stop.
The girl did.

Before Bertrand knew what was happening, she had come up to him and was
saying something in English.   He had
learned very little English, and, in the
surprise of the moment, that little forsook
him.   He simply lay and gazed at her,
feeling as if a fairy-tale had come true.

His silence troubled the little girl, who
took it to mean denial.

She had asked him if he would like a
few wild flowers, and he did not say yes—
he just kept still and looked at her with his
big, strangely sorrowful eyes.   He must
think her rude to speak to him when he
did not know who she was.   It was horrid
of him not to answer !   Her lips began to

tremble ; her cheeks turned red ; she put her hands up to her face, and would have run away, if a sudden intelligence had not come to the boy.

He caught her two hands and pulled them down from her eyes.

"Look at me!" he commanded; and though he spoke in French she knew what he meant. She looked at him, and the smile on his face passed to her's. She held up the wild flowers with a questioning gesture ; he took them with a gesture of thanks. They were friends !

Long after the pink hat had disappeared among the trees, Bertrand gazed down the empty road. He held the little bouquet tight, and now and then stroked one of the flowers gently.

"Will Monsieur go further?" asked Gervase at last. He had been waiting for orders, and was tired of standing in the sun.

Bertrand roused himself.

" No," he answered, " I will go home now."

The wheel-carriage was going slowly along the road when the ladies passed the château on the following day. Bertrand looked at the little girl, and she looked at him, both smiling shyly. Again, she whispered to her mother, as they drew near ; and then they came up to the carriage together.

" May I introduce myself to you ? " said the lady, speaking in French, and in a very sweet voice ; " My name is Mrs. Vaughn, and this is my little daughter Ellen. We are staying for a time at the Villa Claire. My Ellie is lonely here because she knows no other young people. If it would not be troublesome to you, it would give her pleasure to see something of you."

Bertrand raised himself on his elbow, with an effort that brought the blood to his face, pulled the cap from his dark curls, and made her a graceful little bow.

"To see and talk with Mademoiselle—
that will give me great pleasure," he
answered.

"May I bring her to see you, then?"

Bertrand's eyes glowed at the very idea.

"If you would do me that kindness!"
he said tremulously. This fairy tale was
really coming true—more and more so!

"We will come at any time you choose,"
said the lady.

"To-morrow, then, at this time!"

Mrs. Vaughn smiled.

"We will come." She bent her head
in farewell, and the little girl bent her's.
But as the boy gazed after her, she turned
and suddenly kissed her hand to him.

That night, Bertrand could not sleep
for a long time after he had gone to bed.
To understand why the making acquaintance with the little American girl was so
exciting, one must remember the great
loneliness of his invalid life, shut away
from all other children and debarred from

the amusements of his age.   He had
positively never seen a little girl to speak
to before, and was in some doubt as to
what he ought to say and do when she
should come to see him next day.   He
had a general impression that little girls
were extremely shy and easily frightened,
and that you had to speak softly to them
and let them have their own way.   This
last was not a hard prospect as regarded
Ellie Vaughn, for her own way was likely
to be a pretty and harmless way ; but the
curé had told him that in history the
greatest troubles had been caused by
Kings letting silly, selfish women do as
they liked ; so the female way must be a
bad one sometimes.   To be sure, the
curé did not think much of women, and
very likely did not think much of little
girls because they would be women if
they lived to grow up.   He hoped Ellie
would live to be a woman ; she would be
such a sweet, gentle, beautiful woman !

Her way would be a way of mild and loving rule—(for Bertrand was thinking of her as a Queen) and all her subjects would be the better for obeying her. Then, he seemed to see her sitting on a carved throne, with her people about her, and giving commands ; and he was there, not a sickly lad, but a strong knight, and he was going forth to fight for her— to make her enemies bow before her. In fact, poor, tired, worn-out Bertrand had dropped asleep !

When Mrs. Vaughn reached her little villa after the talk with the young heir of Montarbre, that morning, she called Ellie to bring her French reading-book.

" If you want to make friends with this boy, you must be able to say something to him," she said.

" But I don't believe I can learn enough French to talk to him in it to-morrow ; do you, mother ? " Ellie asked anxiously.

" Well, no, perhaps not, Ellie," her

mother admitted, smiling, "but you can go over the little bit you know already, and learn a few phrases, and so feel rather more at home than if you knew nothing at all of his language. Your father and I wanted you to improve your French particularly on this trip, and we have not done much about it yet, have we?"

Ellie blushed; she was not fond of lessons, and she disliked languages especially.

"Don't you suppose he talks any English?" she asked.

"I don't know, dear. It seems to me an excellent idea for you to teach him English, and for him to teach you French!"

"That might be rather fun," said Ellie, with a brightening look.

So she bent bravely to her French Reader, and by dinner-time had learned a page of "polite phrases." Her mother was much pleased at seeing her work in earnest, and hoped that the acquaintance might do more than one thing for her daughter. Ellie was a lovable child, but a very dreamy one. Her father used to say that she walked in a dream, and indeed, the every-day affairs of life had not much interest for her.

She loved to read fairy tales, and poetry, and legends. She liked to "make believe" things, and fancy herself a princess, or a water-nymph, or somebody of that kind, and to tell herself long stories in which she did most remarkable things and had most wonderful adventures.

She was fond of music, and this was the one study at which she had wanted to work hard. In the big American city from which she came she had a number of young friends, and these all thought her a delightful companion because she could entertain them by the hour together with her tales. She wondered now whether the little invalid boy at the châ-

teau would like to have her tell him
stories? She knew he would! But just
then she recollected that he could not
understand her stories, and this was a sad
reflection. She sighed, and took up her
French Reader.

The next morning, long before the
ladies could possibly arrive, all was in
readiness at the château. Bertrand, in
his best clothes, was in the hall to receive
them, and when they had shaken hands,
he asked if they would like to go over
the house. The ladies were very willing,
and the old Antoine, who acted as butler,
proudly escorted them from room to room.
Ellie was awe-struck at the long, shadowy
apartments, the dark tapestries and carv-
ings, the air of gloom and silence and de-
sertion. Mrs. Vaughn for her part, felt the
tears in her eyes as she thought of the
feeble little heir to all this grandeur.

" Has your young master been ill long? "
she asked Antoine.

" Since he was three years, Madame."

" And do the doctors give no hope of his recovering his health ? "

" He will never be better, Madame."

Mrs. Vaughn sighed. She wished her husband were with her, for Dr. Vaughn was a skilful surgeon, and had helped some people as ill as Bertrand.

When Antoine had showed the ladies all that he judged best, they went back to the little invalid, who had been wheeled into his own special sitting-room. Mrs. Vaughn sat down near his chair and talked to him, but Ellie had taken a shy turn and would not say a word. Bertrand was evidently disappointed, and at last addressed her directly.

" I liked those flowers very much, Mademoiselle," he said.

Now was the time for one of the pretty phrases which Ellie had been learning. Alas ! not one could she utter ! She

blushed, and looked down.   Mrs. Vaughn
rose suddenly.

" I am going out to see those handsome
shrubs," she said ; " No—don't come with
me, Ellie : I want you to stay here."

Ellie looked beseechingly after her, but
she went away, and left the two children
together.

Bertrand understood that she did it on
purpose, thinking that her little daughter
would be more at her ease if thrown on
her own resources ; and he smiled.   Then
he held out his hand.

" Come here and tell me the names of
these flowers in English," he said.   " My
English is so poor—I want to learn some
more."

Ellie went to him, and began to talk in
her own natural way, quite forgetting to
be shy, and Bertrand lay back among his
cushions, watching her happily and listening delightedly to her voice, whether he
understood what she said or not.   When

Mrs. Vaughn came back after a time, she found them very well acquainted, and talking a droll mixture of their two languages, the mistakes they made leading to merry laughter.

Ellie was surprised to hear that it was time to go, and the boy's face darkened.

"We are coming again, if you would like to see us," said Mrs. Vaughn.

Bertrand's look left no doubt of his liking to see them, and he begged them to come every day. Mrs. Vaughn thought this would be too often ; but very soon it became the rule.

"Bertrand will not be able to eat any dinner if I don't go to see him to-day, Mother ; " Ellie would say. " He does n't feel hungry unless he has me to tell him a story before he has his food."

Mrs. Vaughn laughed at first at this fancy, but there was truth in it. The disappointment of waiting in vain for his little friend gave the boy a bad headache more than once, and his faithful old nurse, Nannette, came, the third time it happened, to beg that "Mademoiselle might at the least come and speak a few words each morning, when she went for her promenade, since M. Bertrand worried himself if he did not see her."

Mrs. Vaughn was alone, and made the woman sit down and tell her all about the boy. Nannette was very willing. At first, she had not wanted these strangers to come to the château, but now that she had studied them, and found how much better her darling's spirits were for having a companion near his own age, she was anxious to have him see as much of them as possible.

"And he has so few joys, my little master!" she said, wiping her eyes. "No one but me knows what he has suffered, the little angel! and always so patient— so good." 'I will try to be quite still,

Nannette,' he has said with the tears running down his cheeks for pain; 'I am a De Lys, and the men of my house have always been brave.' But the loneliness is worse than the pain."

" I suppose his father feels the child's illness very keenly?" asked Mrs. Vaughn.

" But terribly, Madame! Still, it is not the same with a man as with a woman; the woman stays close to the child that suffers, and suffers, too. A man—well, Madame knows that a man tries to forget! Still, M. le Marquis does everything for M. Bertrand—everything." She looked sharply at the lady to see if she had said too much. Mrs. Vaughn seemed not to notice the look.

" I suppose a great many doctors have seen the boy?" she asked.

Nannette raised her eyes to the ceiling expressively.

" But thousands of doctors!" she answered.

"And have none of them done him any good?"

Nannette began to shake her head in a mysterious way. At the same moment Ellie came into the room, and the nurse said she must be going.

Mrs. Vaughn was sorry the conversation had been interrupted, but she did not think best to talk of Bertrand's illness before her daughter, so she asked no more questions.

On the morning of the following day, Ellie sat beside Bertrand's wheel-chair on the terrace at the château. She had been telling him one of her wonderful stories, and he had praised it.

"You are very clever, Ellie," he said in English.

Ellie colored.

"Oh, no, Bertrand!" she protested, "I'm not at all! I am sure you could tell me a great deal better story than that if you liked!"

13

Bertrand smiled his sweet, wistful smile. He looked curiously at her.

"You really want me to tell you a story?" he asked.

"Oh, yes, indeed I do! Please begin!"

"It will be a true story."

"A true story?" Ellie preferred fairy tales about dragons and dwarfs and enchanted princesses, and such things.

"Aren't there any adventures in it?" she asked anxiously.

Bertrand still looked at her with the expression that puzzled her.

"I don't know," he said slowly.

"Well, tell it, anyway," begged Ellie, coming nearer and resting her elbows on the arm of his chair and putting her face in her hands, as she was fond of doing when listening.

"Very well,—once upon a time there was a château on a hill, with big trees growing thick all about it—— "

"Why, that is like this one!" Ellie
interrupted.

Bertrand went on quietly. " And in it
lived a powerful noble named Noel the
Strong. He was fierce and pitiless, and
the poor hated him. One day he caught
a wretched peasant stealing a hare out of
a trap in the forest. The man begged to
be let off, and said he had a sick wife and
a number of little ones who were starving :
that that was why he had taken the hare.
Noel cared nothing about the man's starving children. He ordered his huntsmen to
beat the poor peasant so terribly that he
never was able to walk again. And the
legend is, that as Noel rode away, leaving
the man bleeding on the ground, the man
raised himself on his arm and solemnly
cursed the wicked noble. ' As thou hast
made me a cripple,' he said, (for he knew
he should never be able to stand or walk
again) ' so shall the son God will send
thee be one, and thy son's son, and in all

the days to come shall there be a cripple in thy house.' And it has been so," Bertrand said in a strange, low voice; "Ever since that day, there has been a cripple in our house." He stopped abruptly.

Ellie had grown quite pale.

" Oh, Bertrand!" she said. And then they sat still and gazed into each other's faces. Ellie had never been so much shocked in her life. She could hardly believe the story; and yet Bertrand's manner showed that he thoroughly believed it himself.

Then a bright idea came into the little girl's head. In the weird stories of spells and enchantments she knew, there was always a charm somewhere by which the spell could be broken—the enchanted prince set free. Her pretty face glowed with hope and enthusiasm, as she leaned toward the boy.

" Oh, but I am sure that that is not all !

Tell me the rest—tell me how the curse can be taken away ; it always ends well, you know, when you find the charm to undo the spell ! "

Bertrand looked at her oddly.

"You certainly are very clever," he said slowly. " Yes, you are, Ellie ! How did you know that there was any more of the story ?   The end of it has come true, I think ! "

Ellie shook her head.

" The end is not until you get well ! " she said firmly ; " but why don't you tell me the charm ? "

Bertrand looked away from her, out over the beautiful view.

" You guessed right," he said ; " there was a charm.   The curse would be lifted when a young maiden from a far country should take it away of her own free will.   Perhaps you are the maiden, Ellie ! "

He tried to laugh, being afraid he might

cry. Ellie threw her arms around his neck and burst into tears.

"Oh, Bertrand, I—I—I 'd do anything to make you well!" she sobbed.

Bertrand was trembling with a new sensation. He kissed Ellie gently.

"It is good to have anyone care so much," he said, hoping she did not notice the sob in his voice.

Ellie sat up again, eager and unsatisfied.

"But you still don't tell me how the spell can be broken!" she cried.

She now believed the legend perfectly. "I want to begin to break it!"

Bertrand was older than most boys of his age, and he had a deeply thoughtful nature.

"I think you are breaking it now, Ellie," he said tenderly.

Ellie almost stamped her little foot.

"I don't know what you mean!" she said.

"Why, before you came, I was discontented and unhappy and cross. And now I am not discontented; I am very contented ! Is n't that -the breaking of a spell ? "

" No, it is n't ! " she replied ; " I want to know what has to be done to make you well, so that you can walk, and do everything ! "

Bertrand looked gravely into her flushed face.

" I shall never be well," he said simply and bravely.

Ellie's eyes grew wide with dismay. The story was so real to her that she could not accept any but the proper ending.

" You *shall* be well ! " she cried, and gave Bertrand a fervent embrace, and fled home to her mother.

Mrs. Vaughn was astonished to see her little daughter come flying into the room in tears. She drew her to her side, stroked her hair, and got her to tell the tale of what had so disturbed her.

" I am very sorry for you, dear," she

said, "and I am more sorry for our dear Bertrand. I am afraid there is not much chance of his being able to walk any more, but, as you are so unhappy, I will tell you something that I was keeping for a surprise. Your father will be here next week!"

Ellie loved her father so much that she almost forgot about her friend for a moment. But it was only for a moment. Her mother went on,——

"And that is not all, Ellie. Your father is what is called a "specialist" for the sort of illness Bertrand has. I do not want you to say anything about it to anyone, but I think your father may be able to help this dear boy—if not to cure him. I do not *know* that he can, but I *hope* it. Dry up your tears, darling, and be brave, whatever happens."

Ellie could scarcely wait till Dr. Vaughn had changed his travelling clothes for another suit, and seated himself in the little sitting-room at the villa, before she told him about Bertrand.

"Oh, Father! you will cure him, won't you?" she pleaded, her arms about his neck.

The doctor kissed his daughter.

"My sweetest, no man can work cures! All we doctors can do is to use the knowledge God has given us as well as we know how. Sometimes the sick person gets well, and sometimes he does not; we do not pretend that all can get well, even with the wisest and best treatment. I want to see your little friend, but you must remember that his father has had the finest French doctors, and that he may refuse to consult me."

"As if any old French doctors knew as much as my father!" Ellie said indignantly.

The next day, Ellie took her father to call at the château. Bertrand looked paler than usual, and the surgeon took a

careful survey of him without seeming
to do so.   He was much interested in
the case, but when Ellie, on their leaving, said, — " There, Father, don't you
think you can cure him ? " he looked
serious.

" I cannot say, dear; I wish the case
were in my hands, but failing that, I can
do nothing."

Two days after, the Marquis paid an
unexpected visit to Montarbre.

Bertrand's letters of late had been all
on one theme, and the Marquis judged it
well to see who these strangers who had
taken his son by storm might be, and what
they wanted.   M. de Lys was one of those
men who seldom credit their fellow-
creatures with unselfish motives.

He listened with a smile to the boy's
description of his new friends.

" Most charming ! " he said. They were
sitting on the terrace, and while they
talked, Ellie came up the avenue.   When

she saw a gentleman she did not know, with Bertrand, she stopped in some embarrassment, and would have retreated but that the gentleman came forward and held out his hand, while the boy called eagerly,—

"Do not go! Do not go! This is my father who wishes much to see you!"

The Marquis made so low a bow that Ellie was astonished.

"Mademoiselle," he murmured in a low voice, "has done me the honor to befriend my lonely child, I am told. Mademoiselle must accept my profound acknowledgments."

Poor Ellie had a fear that he was making fun of her, and felt on the verge of tears. The little heir could not bear to see her look troubled.

"She does not understand what you mean, Papa!" he said to the Marquis softly ; "you are distressing her. Come here, dear Ellie! I am so very glad to see you." He took her hands and kissed them.

Ellie sat down by the familiar wheel-carriage, and felt at home again.

In a few minutes the doctor joined them. He wished Ellie to go and walk, but had allowed her to come and speak to Bertrand first. The Marquis talked a little with him while the children conversed together.

The next day he called at the villa. The doctor returned the call at the château. He thought the Marquis seemed uneasy and abstracted. At last he rose to go, but M. de Lys laid a hand on his arm.

"Pardon me, Monsieur! I have something to say to you. I know who you are. I have heard of your skill. Will you take the case of my son and see what—if anything—can be done for him?"

Dr. Vaughn was surprised, not only by the suddenness of this proposal, but by the feeling the proud man showed in his pale, agitated face and choking voice. Before he could answer, the Marquis spoke again.

"I know that this request seems strange, since the acquaintance between us is so recent, and, perhaps, because I have been assured by some of the most renowned specialists that the case is incurable. But I am his father, and he is my only son! My only child! I cling to the least hope. You come from the new world where I hear there are new and wonderful discoveries; I entreat you to do what you can."

Dr. Vaughn was too much moved to reply for the moment, but he took the hand the Marquis held out and grasped it warmly.

And then he went to see his new patient.

It would take entirely too long to tell the story of the months that followed; of how Dr. Vaughn worked to help the little heir; and of how,—very slowly, almost imperceptibly at first,—Bertrand began to recover.

There were times of discouragement when the great surgeon went to and from the château with a grave face, and when the Marquis looked stern and bitter; times when it seemed as if no skill could rout the disease which held the boy in its grasp. At these times, Ellie would neither smile nor speak, but shut herself up in her room and cried.

But Ellie never really lost hope. For she felt sure the story of wicked Noel was true, and that the charm must be real if the spell were.

And she had no doubt that she was the maiden from over the seas who was to work the charm. It made no difference that Dr. Vaughn's treatment was the means; it was a charm—*her* charm just the same. Bertrand had assured her that this was so; and if he did not know, who did?

She made up a little prayer and said it after her other prayers every night and morning,——

"I pray that the spell be broken, and my dear Bertrand may get well."

And by and by it seemed that Ellie's innocent prayer was answered ; for Bertrand got well!

The Vaughn family went back to America, and Ellie and her friend had to say good-by, but they bore it pretty bravely, for Bertrand—as he stood straight and strong, though slender, by her side on the ship's deck, said to her,——

"It will be only six months until I see you again, for my father has promised to bring me to America, you know."

Ellie nodded wisely. "I know."

And then Bertrand drew a long breath.

"Oh, Ellie—if the spell had not been broken ! "

"It had to be ; that is always the end of the story ! "

The boy looked at her with the sweetest smile she had ever seen on his face.

" We have not reached the end of the story yet ! " he said.

THERE was once a poor crippled man who lived in a little hut with an only son. The son was good and industrious and by constant work kept a shelter over his father's head. But one day the faithful son was brought home dead— struck down in the prime of health and youth, and then the cripple was told that he must leave his home, since there was no one to pay the rent.

It was with a heavy heart that the poor man set forth, hobbling wearily along the high road on a pair of rough crutches, his few possessions tied up in a small bundle on his back.

14

By and by he left the dusty road and turned up a path amongst some thick woods which bordered it on the left.

Following the path for some distance, he came at length to a white, hospitable-looking building, but of a grave and quiet aspect, before which stood two men with

shaven heads, and wearing long brown robes. They turned to look at the stranger, so he pulled off his cap and addressed them respectfully.

"Good Fathers, may a tired wayfarer rest awhile on your door-stone?"

"Surely," said the elder of the two; "but you look hungry as well as tired.

Brother Tertius, bring hither a basin of milk and a platter of food for this traveller."

The young monk bent his head, and went to do the other's bidding.

The basin of milk and platter of food looked very tempting to the poor man, so —first folding his thin hands to ask a blessing—he quickly emptied both.

He was about to resume his journey, with many expressions of gratitude, when the Abbot himself, a stout and cheerful-looking person, appeared upon the scene.

The two brethren explained the presence of the stranger, whereupon the Abbot said,—

"Is not a scullion needed in the kitchen? Let this man take the post an' he will."

The cripple was very thankful to accept a position which would give him a home and a living, but he modestly expressed a fear that he could not satisfy the good monks, seeing that he was so helpless and slow as they saw him to be.

"Well, well, man," said the Abbot, "if thy legs be faulty, thou hast hands; and if thy heart be willing, it will set them to work. So get thee to the kitchen and do thy best. We will give thee a week's trial."

The poor lame scullion suited his employers so well that at the end of the week he was asked to stay with them as long as he liked. Brother Rufus, who was of a merry turn called him "Brother All-Work," because he was so willing to oblige and to take the tasks of others upon himself.

As time went on, the monks forgot that Brother All-Work had ever been a stranger. His patient face was always bright, his crutches carried him on a dozen errands in an hour; his poor, worn hands were at everybody's service, and everybody seemed to want some service of them.

It was a marvel how they had ever managed without him.

And it was also a marvel that they did not see how incessant labor was wearing out the always feeble frame.

Brother Marcus, tall, pale, and thoughtful was too deeply absorbed in meditation.

Brother Rufus had always a mirthfully cordial greeting, as he hurried by ; but he was ever in haste. The brethren were all busy, each in his own way. They were holy men, with much thinking and praying to do, and Brother All-Work never would have expected them to notice the tired looks of a poor scullion, or to ask if his back ached, or his head was heavy.

He went hither and thither, day after day, doing their behests, always smiling ; always with the far-away light in his eyes of one who has had a beautiful dream and believes it will come true.

One day another stranger stood at the door of the monastery,—not poor or crippled, but of kingly bearing, and with the air of one unused to beg for alms.

Brother Trophimus, a young monk who opened the door to visitors, trembled at the gaze of the august traveller.

"I come on a mission to this house," said the stranger. "Take me to thy ruler."

His voice was like his face.

Brother Trophimus bowed low, and led the way to the Abbot's study. The stranger passed in without asking leave, and the door was shut.

An hour passed. Brother Trophimus was summoned to his Superior's presence, and he started as he perceived how great a change had come over the Abbot's round, complacent face.

"Let the brethren presently be gathered together in the chapel," said the Abbot.

"Let not one of them be absent," added the guest from the other end of the room, in a tone deep and musical as the vesper bell.

Greatly the brethren wondered, as they trooped in from the fields, or from their cells, where some were meditating and some sleeping, at the summons.

Into the chapel they filed, old and young, Brother Marcus looking as if half in a trance, Brother Rufus curious as a school-boy, each asking of his companions, " What can this mean ? "

Brother All-Work, seated wearily on the kitchen door-step for a moment's rest, watched them wistfully. He would have liked to follow, but the cook would want him presently. He arose, adjusted his crutches, and, with a longing look at the white chapel with the purple tree-shadows wavering across its walls, went indoors.

Brother Trophimus had been the last to enter, and, looking back at the moment, had caught the scullion's glance.

He hesitated. Was Brother All-Work included in the Abbot's order ? Surely not. As he questioned with himself, the first note of the organ struck on his ear, and he hastened into the chapel to his place.

When the chant ended, the stranger advanced to the centre of the chancel, and, facing the expectant throng, threw back the folds of a dark cloak in which his form had been enveloped.

A thrill passed through the beholders. Dazzlingly robed in white, an angel stood before them, the feathers of his mighty wings sweeping about his feet.

In the hush of awe, where every man communed with his own soul, the angel drew from his bosom a pair of golden scales, and laid a golden heart in one of them.

The heart seemed to weigh the scale down heavily.

Then the angel raised his wonderful eyes, and swept the sea of faces before him.

"These scales weigh no earthly and

visible substance," he said.   "They weigh
the love of God in the hearts of men.
If any man love God for a selfish
reason, the scales remain as now.   But
when a man comes who loves Him only
for His own loveliness, the scales are
equal.   Advance now, ye brethren, from
the least unto the greatest, and let your
love be tested, of what sort it is!"

The monks looked doubtfully at one
another.

"From the least to the greatest."

Who was least among them?   No one
seemed eager to take that place, and there
was a pause.   Then young Brother Trophimus advanced and stood before the
angel.

The scales were still unequal, though
the empty one looked a little nearer the
other.

With flushed face, the young man made
his way back.   One after another, the
brethren followed, each standing a moment

before the angel, each stealing away with lowered eyes.

Even Brother Marcus had fallen short.

Even Brother Rufus looked downcast and sad.

And now, last of all, came the Abbot, with none of his accustomed lordly bearing, but with pale face and faltering tread. The angel's brow was clouded, and his eyes burned like lightning, as they rested sternly upon the Head of the Order.

Alas! again the scales hung uneven.

A silence deeper than they had ever before known reigned in the little chapel.

Only the birds sang gaily in the sunshine outside—the birds that had no cause to hang their heads in shame.

Then the angel spoke.

" Are all the brethren assembled here?"

The Abbot looked around, and answered, " All."

" Surely no," replied the heavenly visitant, " One is absent.   Bring him to me."

The monks gazed wonderingly.

Then the Abbot said, " My lord, there is left but a poor cripple who works under the cook in the kitchen. Scarcely is he one of us."

" Perchance," replied the angel, "yet shall ye bring him hither."

Brother All-Work was on hands and knees, scrubbing the floor of the scullery, when to his amazement he saw the Abbot hurrying toward him.

He struggled up and made a low bow. Had he done something for which he was to be reproved ?

" Brother All-Work," said the Superior in a tone of respect, " thy presence is required in the chapel ; come straightway with me."

The scullion looked down with dismay at his soiled hands and mean clothing.

But the Abbot hurried him along, and into the chapel.

The angel saw him enter, and smiled upon him.

"Come hither, son," said the deep voice.

Tremblingly, the cripple advanced upon his crutches, and when he reached the chancel he fell upon his face in mute reverence. His eyes were hidden so that he could not see what all the others marked in wonder — that in the angel's outstretched hand the golden scales hung even.

"Arise, servant of the Most High," said the angel. "Of all these present, thine is the one heart which is right in the sight of God, because thou lovest Him for His own sake, and not for thine own good."

The bright being laid his hand upon the cripple's shoulder, and he stood upright, with no more need of crutches.

"Say what shall be done for thee," said the angel, tenderly gazing upon him.

Brother All-Work lifted his thin, worn face, bright beyond all earthly brightness.

"That I may 'see the King in His beauty'" he murmured.

Then the heavenly messenger folded his strong arms about the cripple's frail body, and, spreading his golden wings, floated up, past the white-robed saints in the eastern window, past the groined arches of the roof, beyond the eyes of all.

SCORPIO, THE SCORPION

MRS. FANE sat in the pleasant dining-room at Fanesleigh, reading the morning mail. There were a number of letters, and some of them, as she saw from the hand writing, from people whose letters were always good reading,—but when she glanced at a longish, thin envelope with an Indian stamp on it, she gave an exclamation, and opened it in haste, leaving all the rest to wait. As she read, she kept ejaculating, " Dear me ! " "Only think ! " " Fancy that ! " until her husband remarked, laying down his newspaper, " I would, my dear, if you would explain what I am to think about."

"Why, it's the most delightful thing!" replied his wife eagerly; "I was just going to tell you, of course, Harry,—the Winsleigh-Fanes are coming home on leave, and they want to take a house here for the summer, and *of course* we can't hear of such a thing, with all our spare rooms!"

"So you want to have the lot of them here, niggers and all?" said Mr. Fane. "All right, Maysie, go ahead!"

At this moment, Bobby, the seven-year-old son of the house, who had been listening with growing excitement, spoke:

"Oh, Mamma! Are they niggers, really? And do they wear feathers and beads, and have bows and arrows, and will they be awfully wild, and——"

"Oh, nonsense, Bobby!" cried his mother. "Don't you understand that your father is joking? The Winsleigh-Fanes are your cousins from India, and what Papa meant is that they will bring their

Hindu servants with them,—though I hope they wont, I 'm sure," she added, " for I can't bear the creatures ; they give me creeps."

" Why ? " asked Bobby.

" Oh, I don't know—they do, that 's all ! "

" But I want to know *why*," persisted the boy.

" Oh, hush—you talk too much, Bobs," said his father lazily. " If I had asked your mother to tell me ' why ' all through our married life, it would have wasted no end of time ! "

" Why ? " said Bobby.

" Because she could n't have told me," answered Mr. Fane quietly.

Mrs. Fane blushed.

" I wish you would n't waste time now, talking nonsense," she said, " I want to know what you think Colonel Fane will want to have for dinner ; you used to be in India, and you ought to know. And what will the child have? There 's another difficulty. I suppose she will eat things I never had to order before!"

"Why?" put in Bobby.

"Bobs, you can go to the nursery," remarked his father without looking at him.

Bobby went, lingeringly, feeling it hard to be banished from the family councils. He was by no means a stupid child, but he had not managed to learn that his incessant asking "why" had something to do with his being sent so much to the nursery.

He was crying when he reached that apartment now, and Nurse looked at him disapprovingly.

"I should think you 'd be ashamed!" she said.

"Well, I are n't," replied Bobby with some spirit; "I did n't do anything!"

"What 's the matter, then?" asked Nurse. "Have you swallowed something the wrong way?"

"*No!*" shouted Bobby in deep disgust.

" I did n't swallow anything! It's just their wanting to have a secret all to themselves, that 's all!"

" If you mean your pa and your ma, Master Bobby, you should speak of them as such. 'They' does n't stand for no more than 'he' or 'she' for a name, as I 'm always telling you."

" I don't care!" growled Bobby.

"' Don't care' was hanged on a cherry-tree," rejoined Nurse calmly.

" Well, let him! I say, what 'll you do when cousin Winsleigh-Fane comes, and his child who eats queer things, and his niggers?"

Nurse turned round from her sewing and looked at Bobby searchingly.

" I should like to know what you mean by that stuff," she said.

" Oh, yes, I thought you would!" cried the boy maliciously. " But you can ask Mamma! I ain't going to tell you any more than that!"

"You are a naughty boy," Nurse replied, "and you just made up that silliness, as I knew you did."

"I didn't! I truly didn't," asserted Bobby, dismayed by this charge. "Mamma got the letter this morning, and it says Colonel Fane is coming here, and Mamma asked Papa what to get him to eat, and what the child was to eat; and Papa says they are going to bring their niggers, and I asked about it, and asked again, just once or twice—and then they sent me out of the room!"

Nurse did not say anything for a minute. Her busy hands lay idle in her lap, and she gazed blankly out of the window. She no longer doubted Bobby's story, but astonishment kept her silent. Then she began to say a great deal, as is sometimes the way when one is excited.

She said she was not going to stay in any place along with no heathen Indians as did all manner of things a body couldn't put up with, and never, not to say, washed their-selves; and no lady could expect it of her.   Her face grew red, and she fell to folding the clean clothes with a fierce energy, while mischievous Bobby looked on, delighted to have roused her so effectually.

Meanwhile, Mrs. Fane and her husband had arranged their preparations for the reception of their relatives from over-seas, and planned the rooms they were to have, the food they would be most likely to require, and the line of conduct to be observed towards the dreaded Hindu servants.

Three weeks after, one sweet June day, a carriage drove up to the door, and de-posited on its steps, first, a tall, sunburned gentleman, and then a pretty though tired-looking lady, and last of all, a slender, cof-fee-colored young man, dressed in white, holding in his arms a very pale little girl.

Mr. and Mrs. Fane hurried out with the

warmest words of welcome, but Bobby, who stood still on the steps, cried in distinct tones,——

"Only *one* nigger!"

"Bobby, come here and say 'how·do you do' to your cousins directly!" called his mother, hoping his speech about the "nigger" had not been noticed. Bobby came forward and held out a hand deeply stained with a variety of tints, he having spent the last half hour in cleaning his paint-box. The Colonel took the hand with a peculiar smile; his wife barely touched it; but the little girl dispensed with all formalities, and kissed Bobby squarely, at which every one laughed.

"Everything in a good beginning," remarked Bobby's father.

"Moti is a genial little creature," Colonel Fane answered, "but awfully spoiled; —at least, I am afraid so. You see, it's almost inevitable in a hill-station like the one she and Polly have been staying at.

All the people petted her and talked nonsense to her, till she grew to think the world was made for her. I can't do anything with her, and Polly is hopeless—lets her run perfectly wild, don't you know. The only person who can manage her a bit is Dilâl."

The Colonel glanced towards the young man in white, whose immovable face gave no sign of knowing that he was spoken of.

"Dear me!" said Mrs. Fane, "only fancy now! But here we are standing on the steps as if we could n't go indoors; and dear Polly and this sweet child so tired!"

They all trooped in and the Colonel, his wife and little girl followed their hostess into the cool, shady parlor. Colonel Fane turned and said something to Dilâl in a strange language; and he instantly disappeared.

"Tell me about him," whispered Bobby,

going up to Moti who had perched herself
on a high chair, and was gazing round the
room with curious eyes.

"About who?" asked the child, still
looking away.

"Why, *him!* repeated Bobby, pointing
in the direction Dilâl had taken.

"There is n't nothing to tell," answered
Moti indifferently.

"Yes, there is: who is he?"

"He is my servant!" replied the small
person, with a comical toss of her head.

"Your servant? Your very own servant? What does he do?"

"Everything."

"Does he take care of you—is he your
nurse?"

Moti nodded.

"I never!" was the boy's comment.

"It's nothing to be surprised about,"
she said with another toss; "does n't people have them here?"

"Oh, yes, only not black ones; we have

them white.   We don't like black servants.
My mamma says niggers give her *creeps*."

Moti's large eyes flashed.

" My servant is good ! " she cried indignantly.   "*Ever* so good !   And if your
mamma has creeps at him, your mamma
is a stupid."

"Why, Moti ! what is the matter,
dear ?" asked her mother anxiously.   The
passionate tones of the childish voice had
reached her ears.   Moti rushed to her and
burst into tears.

"He is a bad, bad, horrid boy," she
cried; "he says Dilál is a nigger, and
that his mamma has creeps ! "

The singular nature of this statement
made the grown-up people laugh.

Only Mr. and Mrs. Fane understood
that their chatterbox of a son had repeated
his mother's speech on the subject of Indian servants, and they exchanged glances
of meaning.

"Go to the nursery, Bobby," said his

father; " it is the best place for boys who
cannot behave like gentlemen."

Bobby lifted his voice in a dismal
wail.

"Oh, I say, Harry, that's a bit severe,
is n't it?" asked the good-natured Colonel.

" Yes, please don't send him away, poor
little fellow," begged Cousin Polly, " I am
sure he did n't mean to be naughty."

" Reprieved, Bobs!" said his father
with a laugh. " If you do it again, though,
you will be court-martialled."

The two children stared doubtfully at
one another after this. Bobby felt that
Moti had transgressed the ethical code of
his set in telling tales; Moti felt that he
was a very rude boy, and a great disappointment as a cousin. But at their age
quarrels are not apt to last, and neither of
the children was of a sulky disposition, so,
when Bobby softly came nearer and said,—

" Do you like puppies? don't you want
to see mine out in the stable?" Moti put

her tiny hand cosily in his, and said, "Oh, how *lovely !*"

"Moti is devoted to Dilâl," said her mother, when the children were gone. "And it is no wonder, for he is perfectly devoted to her. We have had him a couple of years, now, and we know that he is absolutely trustworthy. He does everything for Moti that a white nurse could, and, when she had a dangerous illness last winter, he did not sleep for several nights."

"Only fancy !" said Mrs. Fane.

"Yes, Dilâl is a first-rate fellow," Colonel Fane agreed.

"But don't you ever feel nervous about him ?" asked Mrs. Fane.

"Nervous ?" repeated Cousin Polly a little scornfully, "no, indeed ; why should I ?"

"Oh, I don't know," answered Mrs. Fane with a little laugh, "only I know *I* could n't stand having any one with me

who was n't white.   I suppose it is just a
prejudice of mine."

"That's all it is, and a very silly one,
too," her husband assented; "if you had
lived in India as the rest of us have, you
would not feel so."

The talk turned on Indian ways and
habits, and then in came Moti clapping her
hands in delight.

"What do you think, Mamma?" she
cried. "I 've been seeing the puppies and
the cat and kittens, and Bobby has given
me all the kittens, and one puppy;—a
black one with tan spots!"

"The hatchet is buried, indeed," remarked Mr. Fane to his cousin, the
Colonel.

"My dear Moti, it is time we went up-
stairs and changed our frocks," said her
mother quietly.

The moon was shining peacefully into
Bobby's room that night, when he saw a
small, white figure come in at the open

door.   Its bare feet made no noise on the
carpet, and as it advanced and stood in the
moonlight, it had a startlingly unreal look.
Bobby, happening to be awake at the
moment, but still drowsy, was about to

call for Nurse, when the figure spoke.

"Where 's my servant?" it said in a
distinct and imperative voice.

"Are you Moti? I was 'fraid of you!"
answered Bobby. "What's the matter, and

why do you go barefoot? Nurse scolds me if I do!"

"Where's my servant?" repeated the little girl; and receiving no reply from the bewildered Bobby, stamped her tiny foot on the floor.

"Can't you *speak?*" she went on in an injured tone. "I should think you was deaf!"

"I don't know what you want," said Bobby. "You're so funny, you know! I think you'd better go back to bed, or they'll punish you."

To this friendly warning, Moti paid no attention, but raising her shrill treble, called at its loudest:

"Dilâl! Dilâl! quickly!"

"Now you've done it!" ejaculated her young cousin, and as the sound of hurrying steps came along the passage, he hid his head under the bedclothes. It was so hot there, however, that he was unable to bear it, and, hearing no sounds of scolding or grief, he ventured to look and see what had happened.

In the bright moonbeams stood Dilâl, Moti in his arms. He was talking to her in a soft, low tone, and in a language Bobby did not understand. Presently he carried her out of the room, and Bobby heard the murmur of the two voices in the room which had been arranged for the little girl across the hall. And then he fell asleep.

"What was the matter with you last night?" he asked Moti in confidence after breakfast the following day.

" Nothing, only I could n't go to sleep," replied his cousin.

" Was that why you wanted your servant?"

" Yes, I wanted him to tell me a story to put me to sleep."

' And would he do it?"

" Why, yes, of course!" Moti opened her eyes in wonder at Bobby's question.

"Would n't your nurse tell you one, if you was n't sleepy?"

Bobby laughed derisively.

"She'd say, 'You are a very naughty boy, and if I don't find that you are asleep when I look in again, I 'll tell your papa!'"

Moti gave the little toss of her head which was a habit with her.

"I 'm glad I have a nicer nurse than your's!" she said.

But Bobby was not ready to admit that this was the case, though he thought his nurse severe in some ways. The children got into an argument which was on the point of becoming a dispute, when Cousin Polly came to the rescue with the delightful news that all the good-tempered people in the family were going to drive. At this, Bobby and Moti first hung their heads, and then laughed, and ran to get dressed.

Before his arrival, Dilâl had been the object of all kinds of surmises on the part of the servants at Fanesleigh; but inside a week, he had made them like him, though his lack of English prevented more than a few words of conversation. Cook, who had declared that " for *her* part, she was n't going to make up no unwholesome messes for no black heathens," now said that "as for that Mr. Dilál, he was quite the gentleman, and no trouble at all;" while Nurse, who had hinted that if that sort of person came to live at Fanesleigh, she should be obliged to leave it—now went peacefully forth every day with the tall Hindu walking at her side, their young charges running before. Even the little girl who helped wash the dishes under Cook told her village friends how interesting it was to hear about India from "that fine, nice-spoken young man," though Dilál's descriptions of his own country were chiefly answers of one syllable to the servants' curious questions.

Perhaps the only inmate of the house who did not like Dilâl was Mrs. Fane, who was a person of prejudices, and who continued to have " creeps."

Bobby, who had an admiration for the Hindu, was rather troubled at his mother's feeling, which she took no trouble to hide from him.

On one occasion, when Dilâl accidently brushed against Mrs. Fane's dress in passing, Bobby saw his mother pull it hastily away with an expression of annoyance, and, coming to her, whispered,——

" You still have creeps, don't you, Mamma ?"

"Oh, hush, Bobby !" the lady said; " what a child you are !"

But Bobby watched her whenever Dilâl was in the room ; he wanted to understand. Another person who noticed Mrs. Fane's aversion to the Hindu, was her husband.

" I really wish, Maysie, you 'd try and

16

treat that fellow a bit more kindly," Mr.
Fane said to her one day.

Bobby was present, but sitting in the
window with a book, and not noticed by
his parents.

Mrs. Fane laughed.

"Don't I treat him right? Well, I do
the best I can; he makes me so nervous,
somehow!"

"Nonsense," said Mr. Fane.

"Well, he does. I believe I 'm afraid
of him. He is so dark and thin and has
such a fierceness under that gentle manner; he always makes me think of a
scorpion!"

Little ears are sharp ears; Bobby had
heard.

He got up and went softly out of the
room, and up to the nursery floor. Dilál
was seated in the room where Moti slept,
making a neat darn in one of that small
maiden's stockings.

Bobby came across the room and looked

on in silence for a while.   But Bobby was never long silent.

"Why don't Hindu people ever have white faces?" he asked presently.

"I do not know, Bobby sahib." Not a muscle of Dilâl's face moved.

"Do you wish you were white, Dilâl?"

"No, Bobby sahib."

"Why don't you?"

"As the man is made, so is it best for him," was the answer.

"But if you could have chosen, would you have been a Hindu?"

A queer flash came into the dark face.

"I would have been as I am—ay, and no other."

Bobby was still for at least three minutes after this; he had a dim idea that his questions had been too personal. Dilâl kept at his work and never glanced towards him.

"Dilâl, what is a scorpion like?"

"I do not know, Bobby sahib."

Bobby was disappointed to find Dilál so uncommunicative. He went away to find Moti, whose little tongue ran as fast as his own. Moti was in the stable, petting her large family of kittens. Bobby sat down beside her and duly admired the soft, mewing, furry things.

"Why wont Dilál talk?" he asked at length, going back to a grievance in an aggrieved voice.

"He does talk," said Moti, "he talks beautifully!"

"He wont talk to me!"

"You don't know his language," she explained. "What have you been talking about to him? The other day you were rude and asked him a lot of silly questions about why he did n't eat beef and bacon!"

"I was n't rude; I wanted to know why he did n't!"

"Why, of course he can't eat beef on account of the sacred cow; and he hates to be bothered about his religion and asked what he does n't do things for!"

Bobby sat still for a minute, pondering this statement. Then he had recourse to his usual question—" Why ? "

" Oh, how tiresome it is always to say *why!* " said Moti impatiently. " My Mamma says you talk too much, and really, you know, you do, Bobby ! "

Bobby was offended. He walked over to the place where the puppies were kept, and took them out of their box, and began to play with them, turning his back to Moti, who, on her part, threw herself back on the clean yellow straw of the empty stall where she sat with the cats, and began to talk Hindustani to her favorite white kitten. She talked in the low, crooning tone Dilâl used to her when she could not go to sleep, lifting the kitten over her head, the half-dozen silver bangles on her little arms tinkling as she moved.

Bobby resented having any one talk be-

fore him in a language he did not understand; Papa and Mamma always talked
French before him when they wanted to
keep a secret : he had to stand their shut-
ting him out, but he would n't stand it
from Moti, who was a year younger than
he, and who had no business to put on
airs.

"Stop talking that stuff!" he called,
with his back still turned to his cousin.
Moti paid no sort of heed ; she only held
the kitten closer and talked on.   Bobby
felt cross; he was in the mood to pick a
quarrel, and he did not try to check it.

"What is that language, anyhow?" he
continued, as if to the fat brown puppy
on his knee; "it is n't any real language,
is it, Fido?   It's just fit for duffers like
that nigger upstairs !"

Moti's crooning had come to a sudden
stop ; she had caught a word she hated—
a word she never allowed any one to apply
to her beloved Dilâl.

For using it, some of her most devoted Indian friends had been dropped by the loyal little maid,—even a stout captain, who had bought her many boxes of French chocolate.

Bobby saw that he had made an impression, and feeling very naughty indeed, he thought he would make it deeper.

"We don't like *niggers*, do we, Fido? We hate niggers, because they're like scorpions, my Mamma says, and scorpions are *nasty* things, Fido; they bite——"

Bobby got no further, for a small hand came sharply against his mischievous mouth with a stinging slap, as Moti, white with anger, flew to his side. She rained slaps on him; and the boy, bewildered at first, rose to his feet, and, holding his left arm as a guard before his face, put out his right hand to push her away. He had no intention of hurting her, for, however teasing and tiresome, Bobby was too manly to strike a girl, but he pushed her from him too hard, and, losing her balance, Moti fell. As she fell, her head struck the edge of the wooden box where the puppies were kept, and she uttered a piercing scream. Bobby was terrified at what he had done, and was stooping to her, when Dilál came swiftly in at the stable door. Bobby never knew exactly what happened after that. He had an impression of a storm passing over him, and leaving him with his ears ringing, and of Dilál, like a white lightning flash, passing out of the place with the little girl gathered to his breast.

The boy sat stupidly where he had dropped under Dilál's hand, rubbing his forehead and trying to remember just what had occurred.

Presently, steps came along the yard outside, and the groom came into the stable and began to loose one of the horses.

"What's that for?" asked Bobby with reviving interest in life.

"The doctor.   Little girl's hurt awful, they're sayin' up at the house."   The man looked curiously at Bobby.   Bobby's face grew pale.

"If I was some people, I'd get away and keep meself out o' my pa's sight," added the groom with meaning.   "I ain't never seen the guv'nor so put out, not as I remember, not since I've been here ; and he's a very easy-put-out gen'leman, too."

Bobby said nothing for a minute ; then he asked,—

"Where is my papa?"

"Well, when I come out here, he were a-looking for his riding-whip!"   William made answer, with a sly glance.

Bobby got up with a proud straightening of his back, and walked into the yard, and across it, through the kitchen-garden, into the front flower-garden, and towards the house.   He met his father striding down the path.   Mr. Fane looked very stern, and Bobby knew well enough what was in store for him. But he only looked his father in the eyes.

"I was just coming to you, Papa," he said in a voice that rang true, even though it trembled.

"Come in; I have got something to say to you," said his father, turning and leading the way to his private room. When they were inside, Mr. Fane sat down, and Bobby came and stood before him.

They looked at each other in silence, and it seemed as if the father was relieved by what he read in the child's face, for his brow grew smoother.

He flung the riding-whip down.

"Well—what have you to say for yourself, first?" he asked.

"How is Moti?" was the boy's answer.

"Her head is hurt,—how much, we cannot tell till Dr. Moore comes. I am glad to see that you think her state the important thing—not your own punishment!"

Bobby's brown eyes never faltered as he said,—

"I know you 'll thrash me; that's all right; you ought to, I suppose; I 'd just like to tell you all about it, though, if you don't mind, before you begin!"

"That 's perfectly fair," said his father; "you heard me tell you to say what you could for yourself. I always know one thing, Bobby,—you 'll give me a straight story of what you 've done; you are no fibber!"

Bobby's square little shoulders grew yet squarer. He plunged into his tale at once.

"You see, Papa, it was this way; I had been talking to her about that fellow Dilál; and she said I talked too much. And so I got cross, and tried to vex her. I pretended to be talking to the puppy, and I said Dilál was a nigger, and that he was like a scorpion—" Mr. Fane started and Bobby stopped.

" What made you think of saying that, Bobby ? " asked his father quietly.

" Why, I heard Mamma say it ! "

" You were in the room, then ? I never noticed you ! When will you learn not to repeat what other people say in confidence? Don't you know it is the cause of half the big and little troubles of life—this telling the silly things other people say without thinking? Remember that, and try never to do it again. To repeat what is said before you by persons who would not wish their words repeated is dishonorable ! "

" Dishonorable " was a word which Bobby perfectly understood. He grew scarlet.

" Well, go on ; what happened then ? "

" Oh, I said some more—I said scorpions were nasty, and bit—and then,——"

" And then ? "

" Why, she ran and hit me ! " Bobby said rather reluctantly.

" And did my son forget what a gentleman's views are on the subject of hitting back if the other party is a lady ? " asked Mr. Fane.

Bobby's reproachful glance reassured his father even before his eager—" Oh, Papa !   As if I would strike a girl ! "

" But what happened then ?   Get on, Bobby—don't be so long about it ; how did the child get hurt ? "

Bobby now hung his head.

" I tried to push her away, and she fell down."

" And hit her head against the wall ? "

" No, against the box—the big box the puppies sleep in.   I truly did n't mean to hurt poor Moti, Papa !   Only, she slapped me so much I had to stop it, and I stopped it too hard ! "

Mr. Fane bit his lip.

" Well, Bobby," he said after a few moments, " I am not going to whip you, as you did not strike your cousin ; but I really can't let you off altogether, for you have behaved very badly, and made a great deal of trouble. You can go to your room and stay there till I send for you."

Bobby hesitated.

" Papa—please—may n't I see her a minute ? "

" Moti ?   No, she is far too ill ; no one but her mother and Dilal are able to see her at present."

" But I want to tell her I 'm sorry ! " sobbed Bobby, with his fists in his eyes.

" I will have her told as soon as she is fit to hear about anything," said Mr. Fane. " Off with you now !   That 's enough ! "

But the boy still lingered.

" Don't be vexed with me, Papa,—only, won't you tell me what Dr. Moore says about her ? "

" Yes, Bobby, I will ; now, away you go ! "

And away he went, crying softly all the

way.   He did not mind being sent to his room, for he was too unhappy to want to play.   He threw himself face down on his bed, and cried and cried.

After a long while, he heard the doctor's carriage drive up to the house, and the doctor's feet come up-stairs.   He lay still, listening for any sound from Moti's room ; but he heard none.   Then—it seemed an age afterwards—he saw the doctor drive away again.   He was too nervous to keep still, so he walked restlessly about his room, taking up things and putting them down again.   By-and-by the door-handle turned, and his mother appeared.   Bobby rushed to her and looked up pitifully in her face.   Mrs. Fane sat down and drew him on her knee.

" It 's all right, you poor dear," she said gently.   " The Doctor says Moti has not hurt her head badly, but that she ought not to have any kind of fright or excitement, because she is a very nervously ex-

citable child. She had a fit of hysterics
when Dilâl first carried her in—screaming
and crying and going on dreadfully!
Her mother could do nothing with her.
It is a pity to have such a violent temper,
and I 'm sure I 'm sorry for poor Polly, but
we must just humor the child all we can
and not have any more scenes like this
one to-day. Your father surprised me by
coming and telling me that it was my joke
about the man reminding me of a scorpion
that made the trouble. What *does* make
you repeat things so? Just see what harm
you have done by it!"

Bobby leaned his head against his
mother, and cried remorsefully.

"Well, don't fret so," said Mrs. Fane,
kissing his hot cheek, "I think Moti will
be well again in a day or so, and your
father will let you come down-stairs to-
morrow. I'll send you up a nice tea, and
then you must get to sleep and forget all
your troubles."

Moti was herself again in a day,—
sooner even than her aunt had expected ;
and Bobby was duly reconciled to her,
after a humble apology.   The whole matter passed from the minds of the family
in a week, and, as Moti's birthday fell
about this time, it was resolved to give a
children's garden-party in her honor.   She
had the choice of what she liked to order
to eat, and promptly decided on strawberry ice-cream, chocolate, macaroons, and
frosted pound-cake,—a selection which
made the mothers look serious.

" You must n't eat all of those, darling,"
said her mamma, putting an arm around
her waist.

" Not all at once ! " Moti agreed ; " just
a bit of each at a time."

" But, my precious, you would have in-
digestion that way, even !"

Moti's lip trembled.

" You said I could have exactly what I
liked !"

"Anything but another fit of hysterics!" said Mr. Fane, who stood by. So the dangerous meal was ordered, to the huge delight of both children.

The birthday dawned fair and warm. Moti rapturously opened a number of parcels, and found a doll in one; a lovely toy parasol in another; a box of paints; a fairy-book; a necklace of Indian silverwork; and a trinket-case of beautifully carved sandal-wood from Dilâl. The little girl was radiantly happy, and flew up and down the house like a humming-bird.

The party was to begin at three o'clock, and long before that time the children were ready and impatient for their young friends to arrive.

"Don't you hate your best clothes?" asked Bobby, as they sat on the cool veranda waiting. He twisted his neck stiffly in his clean collar as he spoke, and looked ruefully at his new knickerbockers in which he was forbidden to climb trees.

Moti cast a fond glance over the soft Indian-silk dress of pale pink, which she was wearing for the first time, and answered,——

"No, I like them!"

Bobby gave a grunt of disgust.

"I'm jolly glad I'm not a girl!" he said.

"Girls are the best things to be, though," Moti averred. Bobby took up the argument eagerly, and it was growing a little too keen for good humor, when the three children of the village doctor happily appeared, putting a stop to it.

"I know we are ever so much too early," remarked the doctor's small son, cheerfully, "but I wouldn't wait any longer. What are we going to eat?"

His two sisters blushed, and the eldest shook her head at him.

But Moti was more than willing to unfold the bill of fare at once.

"We are going to have strawberry ice-cream, and hot chocolate, and macaroons, and frosted cake !" she said proudly.

The doctor's son wanted to know when tea was to be ready ; but at that moment the grown-up people came down-stairs, and led the way out upon the lawn, where croquet and tennis were to be played. Soon the vicar's children appeared, and after them the little Fosters, and all the other young folk who had received invitations ; and a very merry set they were.

The boys ran races, and when the front garden and its lawn was exhausted, Dilâl and the maids brought out tea and laid a charming feast on tiny tables.

To judge from the rapid disappearance of all the good things, Moti's selection was a wise one ; but when the doctor's son passed his plate the fifth time for strawberry ice-cream, and the vicar's three-year-old daughter demanded " more dat sugary cake" at the end of her third slice, the parents present exchanged looks full of meaning, and wondered what would be the state of these young people later.

It was judged best to sit still a while after so hearty a meal, and a game of questions was proposed, the players to seat themselves in a ring on the grass. Bobby happened to hate this sort of game, and his indulgence in every one of the dainties provided had not depressed his spirits.

He therefore beckoned to the doctor's son, who was a crony of his, and, unobserved by anyone, they stole away, and around to the back of the house.

"Oh, are n't I glad we got away !" said Bobby, laughing; "the idea of playing that silly thing ! Let's have a lark, Jack !"

"What kind of one ?" inquired Jack.

"Oh, let's go down on the river bank, and have a swim !"

Now, Bobby knew perfectly well that his father would never have allowed him to go in swimming alone, for the river had a very swift current, and he **had** never gone rowing on it without his father in the boat.

But he put the conviction of his naughtiness out of his head. He had been on his good behavior all the afternoon, and he felt a wild desire to make up for it now. He put his hands to his neck and tore off the linen collar. His pretty suit followed; everything was flung in a heap on the bank, Jack rapidly undressing a few feet away. Then the boys sprang into the water with a laugh.

"Oh—but it's cold enough!" cried Bobby. "Let's strike out hard, and get warm!"

They were both good swimmers, but Jack was the better. At first it was great fun. Swimming was wonderfully easy when the current helped so much; but when they tried to turn and swim the other way—it was a very different matter. They struggled and struggled, and yet it was plain that they kept very nearly where they were in the water. And then, a terrified cry came from Bobby's lips,—for the worst danger of any to the bather had taken hold of his little helpless body—the cramp!

"Yell, Jack!" he cried piteously. "Yell all you can! I can't do a thing for myself!"

Jack needed no second bidding; his screams rang out sharp and clear on the soft summer air.

Very soon after the boys had left the rest of the party, Moti found it out. She was a young lady who expected a great deal of respect, and it vexed her that her Cousin Bobby should leave her on her birthday.

With a funny, imperious little gesture, she called the faithful Dilâl who was watching in the background, to her side.

"What is the wish of Missy sahib?" he asked, bending his six feet of spotless white muslin to a level with her eager face.

" I wish that you find Bobby for me ! "

If any change of expression ever came into the Hindu's still face, a slight curl of his lip at mention of Bobby's name changed it now.

" I had not seen that Bobby sahib was absent," he said calmly.

" He is very bad to be absent ! " Moti said, and there was a sob in her voice which made Dilâl angry with its cause.

" Bobby sahib is a *Budmash*," he replied, " He is always bad." For the servant had not forgiven Bobby either his pushing his little cousin and making her fall, or the title of " Scorpion." Bobby was not sensitive, but he was aware of Dilâl's dislike, and kept away from him.

Moti had told him all that Bobby had said on that unfortunate afternoon, adding that her *Aunt Maysie* had said that he was like a scorpion.

"Very well," Dilâl had said to himself, deep down in his passionate heart, "they call me bad names! It may be I shall deserve them! Scorpion sting; Dilâl may sting too! It is not good to put a stranger in a strange land to shame; he will not forget."

But his Missy sahib liked this bad Bobby, odd as it was. And, to the devotion of the man, this was enough to protect the *Budmash* ("Evil-walker") for the present. So he now asked submissively,—

"Missy wants me to go and bring Bobby sahib to her?"

"Yes, Dilâl, bring him."

The tall, white-robed figure moved away. He had no notion where the boy might be; that was no matter, he would look till he found him. Bobby was not indoors, he discovered. He came out again, into the back garden, and, as a sudden thought struck him, he turned down the pretty path to the river.   And then, in another minute, he heard a scream, and made haste.   There were more screams. He hurried in the direction they came from, and pushing through the young trees which grew thickly along the bank, —saw, first a naked, shivering boy, just come ashore, and then a second boy, tossing his arms as the current bore him down and away.

Dilâl took no time to think.   In an instant he was in the water, and swimming after the drowning lad.   Poor Jack, seeing help arrive, stopped screaming, and watched Dilâl's wide strokes carrying him to Bobby's side.   Now Bobby sank—now he rose ; Dilâl had him—No, he had n't ! Jack shut his eyes.   Then he heard a cry, and saw Dilâl swimming back, slowly, but surely, with the figure of his playmate.

It took a long while, even for the strong man, and when he got to shore, he was

too much exhausted to speak.   The current had beaten him off and pushed him
from the side he must reach.

Ten minutes later, a strange and
sorrowful-looking little procession came
across the lawn to the ring of game-play-
ers.   At sight of it, all sprang to their
feet.

"Oh, what has happened to my boy?"
Mrs. Fane shrieked, running to meet the
dripping white figure that bore a dripping
child.

Dilâl said nothing.   He looked in her
face with a curious expression, and laid
Bobby, wet and unconscious, in her arms.

Two hours after, when all the frightened little guests were gone, and the terrified Moti had been soothed to sleep with
the assurance that her cousin would be all
right in the morning; when Bobby himself, rolled in blankets, and comforted with
hot drinks, was sleeping,—Dilâl sat by the
tiny bed which held his Missy, and thought.

"Yes, that is the best," he was thinking, "to give good for evil, not evil again. It would have been bad to do otherwise. The *Mem*, [Mrs. Fane,] she did not like Dilâl : she said hard words of Dilâl ; she call him *scorpion*. But when he bring her the son of her heart, she not say hard words. She not mind touching Dilâl's hand ; she weep, and she say—' God bless you, Dilâl—so !' " He looked tenderly at the face of Moti.

"And she—she, my little pearl, [1]—she like Dilâl the more ! Bobby sahib bad boy, but Dilâl is glad he is safe. Better so."

[1] " Moti " means " Pearl."

SAGITTARIUS, THE ARCHER

HE little lord of Wilhelmsburg was nine years old. He stood at a window of the great castle where he and his mother had been left while his father followed the Emperor Frederick to the Crusade, and looked longingly out into the green forest. He wanted to be out there with his new bow and arrows.

At a table heaped with heavy books sat a grave-faced man in a black robe, reading.

The boy came up to him.

"Father Johann!" he said impatiently,

"can I not go out now? The sun is drying up all last night's rain."

The man in black looked up with a smile.

"You find it a hard task to wait?" he said.

"It is growing so late!"

"Not very late, my son. And you have not yet paid your respects to your lady mother."

"I will go to her at once."

"You have not yet been called to her presence."

Lord Conrad tapped his foot upon the oak floor. A frown came on his young face.

"It is tiresome to be kept in a leash always, as the hounds are kept," he muttered. "But some day I shall be a man, and then I shall be free."

"To be able to control one's self—that is the only true freedom," said his tutor.

Conrad could make no reply, for at this

moment the door was opened, and a servant announced,—

" The Duchess awaits his lordship."

The boy's brow cleared, and he ran to his mother's room with a light heart.

Lady Hildegarde lay upon a couch, her eyes full of loving welcome.

" A hundred birthdays be granted thee, my son ! " she whispered, tenderly pressing him to her breast, and kissing his cheek. " See what I have made for thee."

She held up a silk scarf beautifully embroidered, and fringed with gold.

" It is splendid, Mother ! Shall I bind it on my arm like a favor ? Yes—and then I shall be your knight, to fight for you ! "

He fell, laughing, on one knee, and the Duchess, leaning over, tied the scarf about his velvet sleeve.

" My little knight ! " she said tenderly.

At that instant the baying of dogs was heard from the courtyard below, and Conrad sprang to the window.

"Hubert is ready! Hubert is waiting for me! I must go to shoot with my beautiful new bow. Oh, Mother, you don't want me to stay, do you? I am longing to try my arrows."

The Duchess looked wistfully at his eager face.

"Go, my son, if Hubert is ready," she said, but a bright tear fell, as she looked after him.

Half an hour afterwards Conrad stood leaning on his bow in a forest glade. He looked discontented and vexed. Old Hubert was picking up the three arrows which he had lately shot, and which had, this time, and each time before, missed their target.

"You don't know how to shoot," said a strange voice near by.

Conrad turned sharply, and saw a strongly-built lad of about his own age, brown-skinned and brown-eyed, with shabby clothes and bare feet.

"Who are you?" asked the young heir of Wilhelmsburg angrily, "and how dare you say that to me?"

"I am Dolf Schmidt, and I always dare tell the truth," replied the stranger with a coolness which made the other more angry.

"Take that, then!" cried Conrad, striking at him fiercely.

"And take you that!" said the sturdy Dolf, calmly prostrating his enemy on the grass.

A moment after, a big hand lifted the brown-faced boy, shaking him as a dog shakes a rat.

Hubert had hurried back as Conrad fell, and seized Dolf in an iron grasp.

"Wretch!" cried the old huntsman, I'll soon teach you how to treat your betters!" His heavy dog-whip swung threateningly in the air as he spoke.

Dolf looked at it, and set his teeth. He would not beg for mercy. He would not utter a cry or shed a tear.

18

But as the lash came down on his half-naked back, Hubert's arm was stayed. Conrad had risen and come to the rescue.

"Stop, Hubert!" he called commandingly. "He meant no harm, and I struck the first blow. Here, Dolf Schmidt! Take my bow and shoot an arrow if you will. I like you."

Dolf said nothing, but he looked at Conrad with sparkling eyes.

Then he took the bow and arrow.

"What shall I shoot at?" he asked.

"That brown bird on the bough there!" said Conrad, pointing to a small object on the top of a tall tree some way off.

"Nay," said the ragged archer. "It were a pity to kill the bird. She has a nest in that tree, it is likely. I will shoot the branch from under her, and not hurt so much as a feather."

So saying, he laid an arrow in place and pulled the string.

The dart fled like a hunted thing through

sun and shade until it struck the twig
under the brown bird. Up flew the startled

creature, unharmed,—down fell the broken
spray. Conrad clapped his hands.

"Good!" he cried generously.

"Very good," said the voice of his tutor, who had joined the group unnoticed.

"And who are you, my son?" said he kindly to Dolf.

"The cowherd's boy, Father," Hubert interposed.

"And how came you here?" went on Father Johann to the child.

"I was going home, and stopped to watch the young gentleman shoot."

"And to tell the young gentleman that he did not know how?"

Dolf blushed and looked down.

"Never mind," said Conrad, his cheeks as red as the others'. "He is right. I do not shoot well, and he does. Courage, Dolf! Here is another arrow."

"I must go now," said the cowherd's son. My father will scold me. Good-day, sirs!"

He made a gesture of respect, and turned to go.

"Come again to-morrow!" called Conrad.

"Yes," said Father Johann.

"It will be an excellent thing for Lord Conrad," said Father Johann to the Duchess that evening. "I know the child's parents. They are decent, honest folk, and the boy is like them. It is written in his face."

The Duchess looked doubtful.

"I reverence your judgment, Father," she said, "but my darling boy—can a rude peasant lad be a fit playmate for one brought up as he has been?"

"Dear lady," replied Father Johann, with his winning smile, "it is exactly because of the way your son has been brought up that I think Dolf a good companion for him."

"At least, you will not leave them alone until you have studied the boy carefully!"

"I promise that," said the tutor willingly.

Dolf presented himself at the castle on the day following. His mother had made him fine with an old red necktie, and had combed his tangle of black curls, and scrubbed his face till it shone.

But Dolf was aware of many drawbacks, —his ragged sleeve—his bare feet, and when a big man-servant ushered him into the present of the Duchess herself, he could hardly lift his eyes from the floor.

The lady soon sent him away, pitying his confusion.

Outside the room, alone with Conrad, Dolt found his voice again.

" Is she your mother ?" he asked.

" The Duchess ? Yes, of course."

" She is beautiful as an angel from heaven. You must love her much."

"Of course," said Conrad again, rather stiffly. Then, with a change of tone,— "Come and see the horses ! I will show them to you."

Dolf was ready. Once in the stable,

he crept into the stalls, patting the horses, stroking their necks, talking to them.

"Take care, Dolf!" cried Conrad as the boy approached a powerful black horse placed apart from the rest. "That is a new comer, and no one but the head groom dares to touch him. He is dangerous."

"I dare," said Dolf, setting his teeth. "See!" The little heir watched, pale and frightened, as the black-haired boy climbed to the manger above the horse's head, and softly brought his brown cheek close down to its sensitive right ear.

A moment after, and Dolf's bare legs were astride the creature's unsaddled back, while he fondled the sleek neck lovingly.

In yet another moment he had loosed the tether, and "Emperor" was free.

"How dared you? How did you do it?" whispered Conrad, as if afraid of breaking a spell.

"A secret!" said Dolf smiling. "Now watch me ride around the courtyard!"

" You could not do it ! "

" See ! " Dolf's eyes shone. He tossed the curls out of them, and pressed his feet against Emperor's sides. Away went the bonny black steed, twice and thrice around, and Dolf laughed, and all the grooms ran to the castle-yard at the noise of galloping hoofs. The dogs barked, the women-servants who peeped out at windows screamed—there was a mighty hubbub.

Then the ragged rider checked his steed, whispering into its ear as before, rode it back to its stall, and tethered it fast.

And after that every one began to talk and wonder and scold, and the head groom came up to Dolf with an angry look.

But Conrad stood his friend.

" Be quiet, all of you ! " he cried imperiously. " Dolf Schmidt can ride Emperor if he choose, for he is a better horseman than any man here." And, throwing one arm about his companion's frieze jacket, he led him back to the castle.

Father Johann was hurrying out with an anxious face as the boys entered.

" It is all over !" said Conrad, laughing. " Dolf is best archer and best horse- man.   Now we shall see in what else he excels.   Come up-stairs to my playroom, Dolf! You may play with all my play- things."

He led the way up a flight of winding stairs, into a turret room.   Two pretty silky-haired dogs ran barking to him, and making friends with them, Dolf forgot to be shy of the tutor.

Conrad expected the little cowherd to express great surprise at the beautiful things he showed him, one by one,—things his father had brought from far-away lands, but Dolf cared for nothing so much as the dogs; and presently he was down on the floor, playing with them and teaching them tricks.

"Your horse of chased silver with jewels for eyes is well enough," he said, "but for my part give me something that is alive."

Father Johann smiled when he heard this, but he said nothing. He watched Dolf through the day, without seeming to do so, and he liked the free-spoken lad well.

And it was settled that evening between the Duchess and the tutor that Dolf Schmidt should come and live at the castle, and be trained for Lord Conrad's body-servant.

The scheme suited everybody.

To be sure Dolf rebelled at first against hose and shoes, and fretted sadly that he could not climb trees in his new clothes.

He broke all bounds at times, and returned from truant expeditions into the woods with torn doublet and berry-stained hands.

But these things were only the natural

uprisings of a brave and hardy nature, and he was soon restored to favor.

The worst piece of mischief into which he fell was the prompting of Conrad to a boating excursion in an old barrel on a deep pond in the forest. This adventure nearly cost both boys their lives. Lord Conrad, by his wilful desire to steer the odd craft,— a desire which Dolf resisted with muscular force,—overturned the barrel in mid-ocean, and only his young servitor's presence of mind and ability to swim saved him. Dolf was nearly as much at home in the water as out of it, and so managed to bring the little Duke safe to shore though Conrad's struggles made it a hard task.

Happily old Hubert was not very far away, and got them back to Wilhelmsburg with due speed.

This, the gravest of Dolf's misdoings, was also his last. He was severely punished, but his worst punishment was to have Conrad's gentle mother say,—

"I am more grieved than angry, because I trusted my son to you,"—and he
gave himself no rest until, after long per-
severance in well-doing, he one day heard
her say,—"Dolf, I can trust you again."

Ten years passed by, and Conrad was
Duke. His father had fallen in battle,
his gentle mother had died not long after,
and the lad of nineteen was lord of castle
and lands.

Father Johann yet lived, but he was
now very feeble. And Dolf was there—
still bold and daring, but not so rash as
of old.

A true and faithful servant he had
proved, and the young Duke loved him.
But Conrad was the same as he had ever
been ; and a new pleasure could absorb
him now as it had at nine years—a new
friend influence him now as then.

It had fallen that, on a certain summer's
day, a young minstrel, or "minnesinger,"

had come caracoling up to the castle on a piebald pony, and, being admitted to the presence of Lord Conrad, who was in a dull mood, had charmed him with music and merry talk, and straightway won the boy-Duke's impulsive heart. Conrad was young, and the castle lonely and dark and grim, and Ludwig the minstrel knew the way to make time pass right merrily.

So Conrad kept him from day to day, and the days turned to weeks, and still there was nothing said of departure.

Dolf had distrusted the gay stranger from the first. He was too generous to harbor a mean jealousy, and when, on his showing his dislike of Ludwig on one occasion, his master had charged him with such a feeling, his quick temper had led him to make a reply which greatly offended the Duke's pride.

Thus a coldness had fallen between the two which seemed likely to last.

But, though Dolf was hurt, his loyalty to Conrad never faltered. He kept the closer watch on Ludwig the minnesinger, and his mind was busy while he kept silence.

His heart swelled when his old companion's eyes passed by him to beam on the new favorite, but his devotion was unchanged.

Father Johann, confined to his own suite of rooms, was much concerned when the matter came to his ears, and pleaded with Conrad.

"It is all Dolf's jealousy," said the young Duke, laughing. "That fellow is over-pampered, and snaps at rivals like a lady's lap-dog. Believe me, good Father, Ludwig is a friend worth the having. He sings like a bird in June. I will bring him to sing before you, and you will laugh with me at Dolf's dulness."

But somehow, from one reason or another, Ludwig never sang for Father

Johann, and Dolf, keenly noticing his every action, distrusted him the more.

Then, one morning, came the minnesinger to the Duke with a long face, saying that he must tarry no longer, but must forth again to seek his fortune, in three days' time.

Conrad vowed he should not go, but Ludwig vowed that he must, and begged of his kind patron one last mark of favor,—that he would ride with him to the border of his domain,—they two alone.

Now it happened that at this time the country was in a very unquiet state, the barons warring against one another, and the strong crushing the weak underfoot.

Conrad Von Wilhelmsburg had more than one powerful enemy, and the most dangerous was a Count Walther Von Altenbauer, who had long looked on the little duchy with greedy eyes. Count Von Altenbauer was many years older

than the Duke, and Conrad's advisers had
warned him to be ready for some stealthy
attack, but light-hearted Conrad laughed
at danger.

And when the minstrel begged that he
would ride alone with him to the border,
he readily agreed.

Dolf was much distressed when he
learned of it.   He knew that remonstrance
with his master was useless, but he resolved to follow when the two set out.

On the evening before, he went to
Hubert's son, now occupying his father's
place, a stout and sturdy man at arms.

" Look you here, Albrecht," he said,
drawing him aside. " To-morrow, the
Duke rides alone with the minnesinger to
the border. Now, be ruled by me. I
like not this Ludwig—nor do you, I well
know. Have a score of strong fellows,
armed, hid by the hollow oak at the cross-
roads. I myself will follow the riders on
foot, keeping out of their sight, and if I

see aught go wrong, I will shoot an arrow at top of the oak. Dost catch my meaning?"

Albrecht's small blue eyes flashed fire. He understood.

The part of the border chosen by Ludwig was the eastern, adjoining the land belonging to one Friedrich the Black, a friend and ally of Count Walther Von Altenbauer.

The riding path lay chiefly through woods in full leaf, and, as the horsemen passed through them, Dolf was able to keep them in sight whilst half hidden himself.

Conrad was particularly affectionate towards his favorite on this last morning, and his kind words seemed to fall on grateful ears, for the minstrel often raised a saffron-tinted kerchief to his eyes, and bore himself with a melancholy air. But as he neared the border, his spirits seemed to lighten. The watchful Dolf saw him raise his head and glance eagerly about. The two horsemen came out into an open space at the instant, and Ludwig rode on a few paces, suddenly wheeled his horse around, and, riding back, stooped as if to pick up something.   It was the saffron-colored kerchief.

Suddenly, from a low thicket sprang out a dozen armed men and surrounded the Duke.   But, quickly as it all happened, Dolf's arrow was quicker still, as it flew to summon Albrecht and his men to their master's aid.

A second arrow struck the foremost of the enemy, and a third and fourth made a breach through which Dolf rushed, dagger in hand, to the Duke's rescue.

Conrad, recovered from his first surprise, was now fighting vigorously in his own defense, and, with Dolf's help, he kept the Altenbauer retainers at bay until Albrecht's band came upon the scene.

This reinforcement soon decided the

fray, and in a few minutes the enemy were in full retreat.

As Conrad was putting his dagger back in its sheath, two of Albrecht's men came forward with a prisoner. It was none other than the minnesinger, his lute gone, his gay clothes torn, his face pale with terror, as he stood before the man he had betrayed.

Conrad gazed scornfully upon him.

Then he turned to Dolf, who stood apart.

"Come hither!" he cried. Dolf approached with a firm but modest mien.

His young master laid a hand gently upon his shoulder.

"Good and faithful friend," he said, "I have done wrong in trusting a stranger rather than thee whom I have so long known and so often proved. This stranger is now at thy mercy. Do what thou wilt with him."

Dolf's breast heaved, and for a moment

he seemed unable to speak. Then he raised his dark, stern eyes to the captive's face and pointed across the border with the single word, " Go!"

As the minstrel slunk away, Conrad threw his arms about his old comrade's neck, saying,—

" For the future none shall ever supplant thee, truest of friends and best of archers!"

CAPRICORNUS, THE GOAT

N a forest of the Tyrol once lived a poor charcoal-burner with his wife and their only child, a boy of ten.

There were no other children near enough for Hansel to play with but he did not mind this, for he made companions of the wild flowers and the wild creatures of the wood. He liked to watch the birds, the rabbits, and the frisky red squirrels, and he listened to the sounds they made, and imitated them so well that the little wood-folk answered him, and came to his call.

None of them feared him, because he never harmed anything. As he sat on a mossy bank, they would draw nearer and nearer, until the bravest would drop down from a bough upon his head or shoulder, and the others, seeing it, would run up his arms, and perch here and there on his body.

Hansel's mother looked upon the strange power he possessed over animals as something very like magic, and was afraid the fairies had a hand in it, and might carry the boy off to Elf-land some day. So she tied around his neck a pewter medal with the head of a saint on it, and taught him a prayer which he was to say to the saint if ever the fairies tried to bewitch him.

"I wish they would," said Hansel; "I would like to see the fairies."

"Never say that again, foolish child!" cried his mother. "Do you want to be carried off and turned into you don't know what?"

"I'm not afraid of them!" said Hansel.

"Do as I tell you, just the same," answered Gretel Myers sharply.

"Why, yes, Mother, to be sure I will," he said, for he was an obedient boy.

One summer day Hansel sat on a bank under a favorite tree whittling a bit of wood into the shape of a goat. The live goat which he was copying munched the leaves of a vine close by. She was a pretty creature, and gave the milk which made Hansel's black bread taste so sweet at breakfast and supper.

He had finished his model, and was examining it with some satisfaction, when a stranger appeared beside him.

Hansel was startled, but not really alarmed. His first thought was of fairies, but he felt that fairies must be little and gauzy, and would not wear suits of gray cloth, nor carry big white umbrellas, nor have such broad shoulders and long brown beards. Still, he was a very little nervous, for he had not seen many people in his short life.

"Good-morning, my little man," said

the stranger. " I have lost my way in your big tree-world. Can you tell me the road to Ṁ——? "

" My father can," said Hansel shyly.

" And where is your father ? "

" Yonder where the smoke is rising among the trees," replied the boy pointing. " He is a charcoal-burner."

" And you are a wood-carver, it seems," said the unknown, stooping to pick up the wooden goat which Hansel had dropped. " Who taught you to carve, little one ? "

" No one," answered Hansel, blushing and looking down.

" A genius !" murmured the stranger to himself. " Will you take me to your father ? " he added aloud.

The charcoal-burner rose from tending his fire, and took off his ragged cap.

He answered the gentleman's questions as to the way to reach M——, telling him that the village was a good three miles away.

"So!" said the traveller. "I have walked far already and am tired. May I rest at your house before going farther?"

"With a good will," was Carl Myers's hearty response, and, striding along at a swift pace, he soon brought his guest to the rude hut which served him for a home.

Gretel Myers was not a little flustered to have a fine gentleman come in so unexpectedly, but she set a stool for him at the roughly hewn table, placed a clean, coarse cloth upon it, and soon had a blue bowl of milk and a brown loaf before him.

Herr Steiner praised the milk, and the pretty goat that gave it; and then he drew Hansel's carving from his pocket and asked if the child had really never had a teacher.

No, indeed! answered the parents in a breath. They were too poor to do more than clothe and feed their boy, and could give him no schooling.

"That is a pity," observed the Herr, "for he must be a clever boy."

Clever! Gretel was certain that no such a boy as Hansel lived; and she ran to the cupboard and took out a number of his works of art, and stood them on the table proudly, for there might never be such another chance of exhibiting these

wonders to someone who could appreciate them. There were little men and women, birds, rabbits, and squirrels, all, as the mother said, "the very living things themselves."

Herr Steiner looked at each with growing interest. And Hansel, hidden behind his mother, watched him in shy delight.

Presently the Herr looked up.

"Send your little lad out to play a while," he said, nodding towards the door. "I have something to say to you both."

Hansel went out, and walked beyond ear-shot, like the honest little fellow he was.

But he did not feel like play. He sat down under a tree, and wondered what was happening in the hut. He could not help thinking that they were talking about him. He began to feel frightened without knowing why. It seemed as if a long time passed.

Then Carl Myers called him, and he went slowly in, and saw that his mother's eyes were red.

"Get your Sunday suit on, Hansel," said his father. "You are to go to the city with the Herr."

"Mother!" said the boy, looking at her with appeal in his pale face.

"Yes, dearest heart," she said, trying to

smile. "The Herr will make a great man of you, he says. You shall learn to make beautiful statues like the saints in the church at M——, and when you are rich, some day, you shall come and stay with us—always."

Her voice broke at that, and Hansel ran into her arms, and Carl and Herr Steiner went outside and left them together.

In another half-hour, the artist and the boy set out together for M——, Hansel carrying a little bundle in one hand.

There was a big lump in his throat, and the trees swam before his eyes, but he did not shed a tear until he cried himself to sleep that night in his room at the inn.

By and by came a letter from Dresden to the Myers family, giving good news of Hansel. Carl and Gretel walked to M—— to carry the letter to their kind old priest and hear him read it aloud, for they were unable to decipher it themselves.

The next letter was written by Hansel himself—which made them very proud.

Ah! yes—but no one need be surprised at anything Hansel did, the mother declared, stroking the letter softly as it lay on her knee. If ever a boy was cut out for greatness it was Hansel!

The charcoal-burner only smiled at this, but he shared his wife's opinion.

The parents talked of little but their son and his prospects, and every night they went to rest with their hearts full of him.

But as the months passed into years, they began to long for a sight of him.

So the old priest wrote a letter for them to Herr Steiner, begging that Hansel might pay them a visit. And in time came a letter from Hansel announcing that he would be with them at Whitsuntide.

Then Gretel made great preparations,

and there was nothing for a month but
scrubbing and sweeping and mending..

"A poor place, Hansel will think it,
when all is done, after the fine houses of
the city," sighed Gretel; but her husband
shook his head.

"The lad is a good lad—he will be
thinking how happy he was in the old
days. Never fear but he will be glad to
see his home."

And so he was. But the parents stared
when he came springing in at the door
one evening. Could this tall, well-dressed
youth be their own Hansel—the very
same Hansel? He was not long in con-
vincing them, for his arms were about
them, and his voice trembled as he called
them by name.

After he had been kissed and embraced enough, and his height measured
by his father's, he was allowed to seat
himself on the roughly cut stool he used
to sit on, and begin the story of his

adventures in the five years since he left the forest.

His father sat opposite, silently smoking, but his mother drew her stool close beside his, that she might stroke his hand or the fine cloth of his sleeve.

Hansel had so much to tell that it was very late indeed before they retired to rest. He had seen so many wonderful things—such splendid galleries of pictures, and halls full of statues, and had met such great men; for the great men came to his master's studio to have their busts made; and, when some of them died, the city they had distinguished would commission the artist to make a life-size marble or bronze statue.

"And canst thou make a statue?" inquired the charcoal-burner with a smile.

"Why should not the boy make a statue, or aught else?" broke in Gretel sharply. "He could ever turn his hand to anything. Did not the honorable Herr praise the goat he carved on the very day he left us? See, Hansel—here it is, and a right pretty bit of work, too, I say—let who can turn out a better!" So saying, the good soul ran to her corner dresser, and took down the wooden goat, and set it on the table before him.

"What a queer old thing!" the youth said, laughing, as he took it up and examined it. "Did I really do such bad work then? I will carve you a better goat now, if you will give me a bit of wood, little Mother."

And so he set to work straightway, and when he had finished, the parents were obliged to confess that the new goat was finer than the old.

But Gretel's was a faithful heart, and she kissed the clumsy old carving before she set it back on the shelf. She had taken pride in it so long, and it had comforted her when Hansel was far away.

"Old friends before new," was her motto.

When Hansel was starting to go back to the city, he slipped a purse of gold into his mother's work-worn hand.

"Eh, lad—what's this?" she cried, in dismay.

"It is all mine by good right, Mother; the Herr Meister gave it me for you. He says I have fairly earned it."

Gretel clung about his neck, crying. "My boy—my boy—! How can I lose you again!" she sobbed.

"Take heart, little Mother," he whispered, tenderly kissing her. "Some day when I am rich, and have a house of my own, you and the father here shall live with me, and we will all be happy together."

And then Hansel was gone.

He loved his parents, but his life grew more and more full and busy, and though he meant to go back and see them in another year, it passed, and the next, and the next, and he did not go.

He wrote, and his letters were the great pleasure of their life—the lonely, uneventful life of the great forest.

He told of the rapid progress he was making—of the orders for work which began to come in—of the praise he had received ; of medals and prizes.

He travelled in other countries; his letters bore postmarks of Italy, France, England—America.

The good couple were much distressed that their son should go to so far-off and dangerous a place as the last, which they had heard was a land of wild beasts and Indians. They were very glad when they heard of his return to Germany.

Eight years had now slipped away since they had seen him.

And in the summer of this eighth year, Hansel realized his dream of a house of his own—a house fit for a great artist, and one filled with his own beautiful handiwork.

The dining-room was panelled in wood carved by himself, the stair-rail was a great, twisting, twining wild-grape vine. But most charming of all was the stand for the tall hall-lamp. This was no less than a goat, poised in act to spring from a rock—the lamp between its graceful horns.

Yet Hansel had realized but one half of his dream. He had the house, but now he must bring his old parents into it ; and one sunny morning he set forth with a glad heart for the great forest.

" Yes," he said to himself, " I have left it too long already. I must lose no more time. Life is short, and one cannot always have a father and a mother."

He reached the little village on the border of the forest late in the evening, and slept at the well-remembered inn where, as a homesick child, he had cried himself to sleep so long ago.

Early on the following morning, he started alone and on foot for the charcoal-burner's hut.

An unaccountable sadness had come over him, and it deepened as he drew nearer to the old home.

At last he saw it. He took off his hat, and ran towards it, shouting—"Father! Mother!"

But no one answered. No eager faces appeared at the little dark windows.

He pressed on, he entered through the unlocked door. All was empty, silent, and deserted.

The rude picture of St. Hubert was gone from the wall; the plates and mugs from the dresser; the big, coarse linen-covered bedding from the low, rough bed.

A squirrel sprang down and out of the door, into the green world beyond.

Hansel's eyes filled with blinding tears. He flung himself on his knees by the cold hearth, whose dead gray ashes seemed a picture of the desolation of his heart, and laid his head on the old stool.

"God forgive me!" he cried. "God grant I find them yet!"

Then he rose up, and retraced his steps to the village. The priest could tell him all.

The old priest was dead, said the hostess at the inn, but the Herr could see young Father Gottfried—yes, indeed.

So to the house of the Father went Hansel.

The young priest's face grew bright with interest.

The honorable Herr was the son of Carl and Gretel Myers! Ach so! He knew of the honorable Herr's great fame and renown. But where were Carl and Gretel Myers? Truly—had the Herr not yet seen them? They were gone to Dresden a month since, and to see the honorable Herr. Was it possible that some mischance had befallen them?

It seemed too likely.

Hansel could learn little more, but guessing that Father Gottfried had been of much use to his parents, he left with him a sum for his poor which so greatly astonished the worthy man as to leave him nearly speechless.

And now Hansel was back in Dresden, seeking his father and mother.

Three anxious days passed after his return, and then as he sat at dinner in his handsome dining-room, pretending to eat, but too sad to do more than play with what was placed before him, a servant brought word that a pair of beggars were outside, demanding to see the Herr, and refusing to be sent away.

" I have in vain told them that your honor is not to be disturbed.   They insist that your honor open this package."

Hansel seized the little parcel, and tore it open with shaking fingers.

It was the old wooden goat !

"Father! Mother!" he cried, rushing to the door.

Yes,—there they were,—aged, weary, worn,—but the same loving souls as of yore.

"And now we shall be happy together," murmured Gretel, her head on his breast. "The goat has done it!"

THE END

www.ingramcontent.com/pod-product-compliance
Lightning Source LLC
Chambersburg PA
CBHW031029120726
47905CB00007B/2107